A JOURNEY TO MOUNT ATHOS

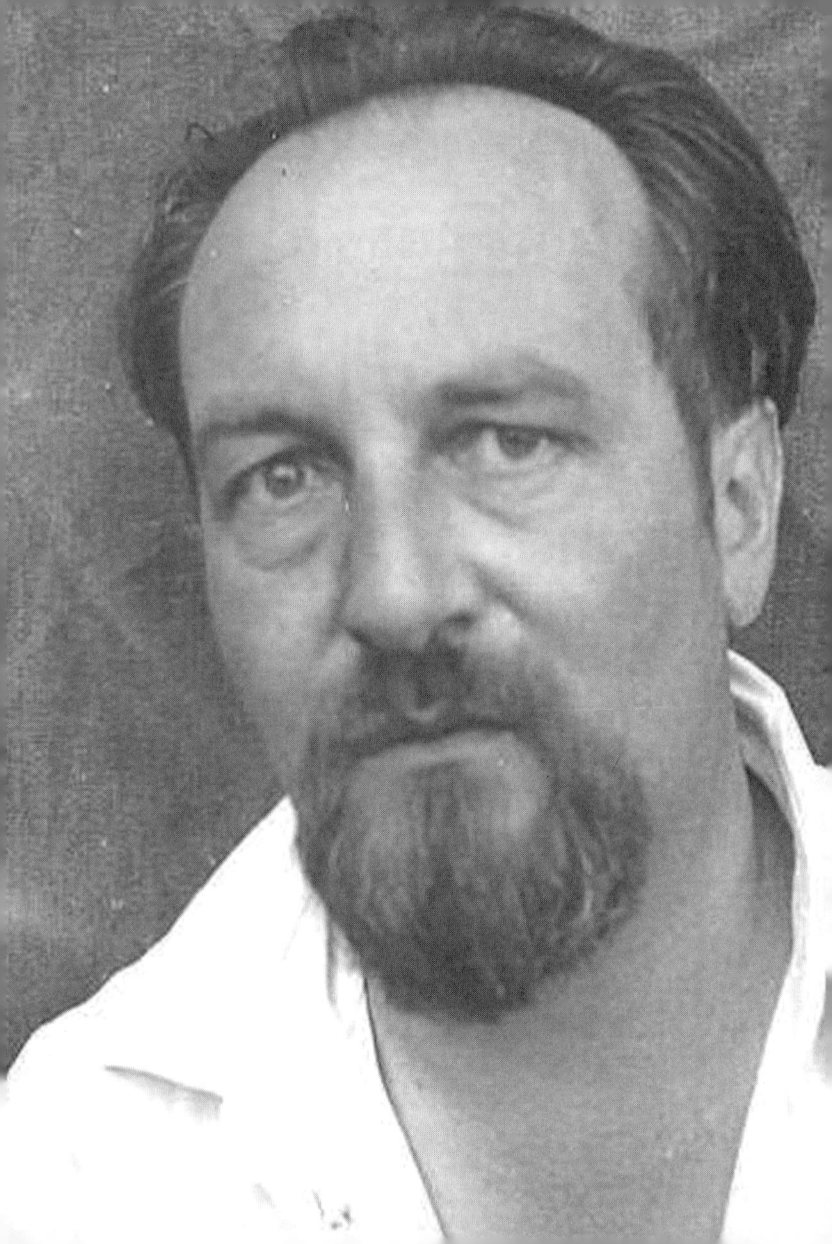

FRANÇOIS AUGIÉRAS

A JOURNEY TO MOUNT ATHOS

Translated from the French by
Sue Dyson and Christopher Moncrieff

PUSHKIN PRESS
LONDON

First published in French as
Un voyage au mont Athos in 1970

This edition first published in 2008 by

Pushkin Press
12 Chester Terrace
London NW1 4ND

ISBN 978 1 901285 39 0

Cover: *Vézère-Falaise dans la nuit* François Augiéras 1957
Courtesy of Association François Augiéras Domme et Sarlat

Frontispiece: François Augiéras 1964
Courtesy of Association François Augiéras Domme et Sarlat

Illustrations by Jacques Lacarrière
from *Mont Athos montagne sainte* 1954

Set in 10 on 12 Baskerville
by Alma Books Ltd
and printed in Great Britain by TJ International

A JOURNEY TO MOUNT ATHOS

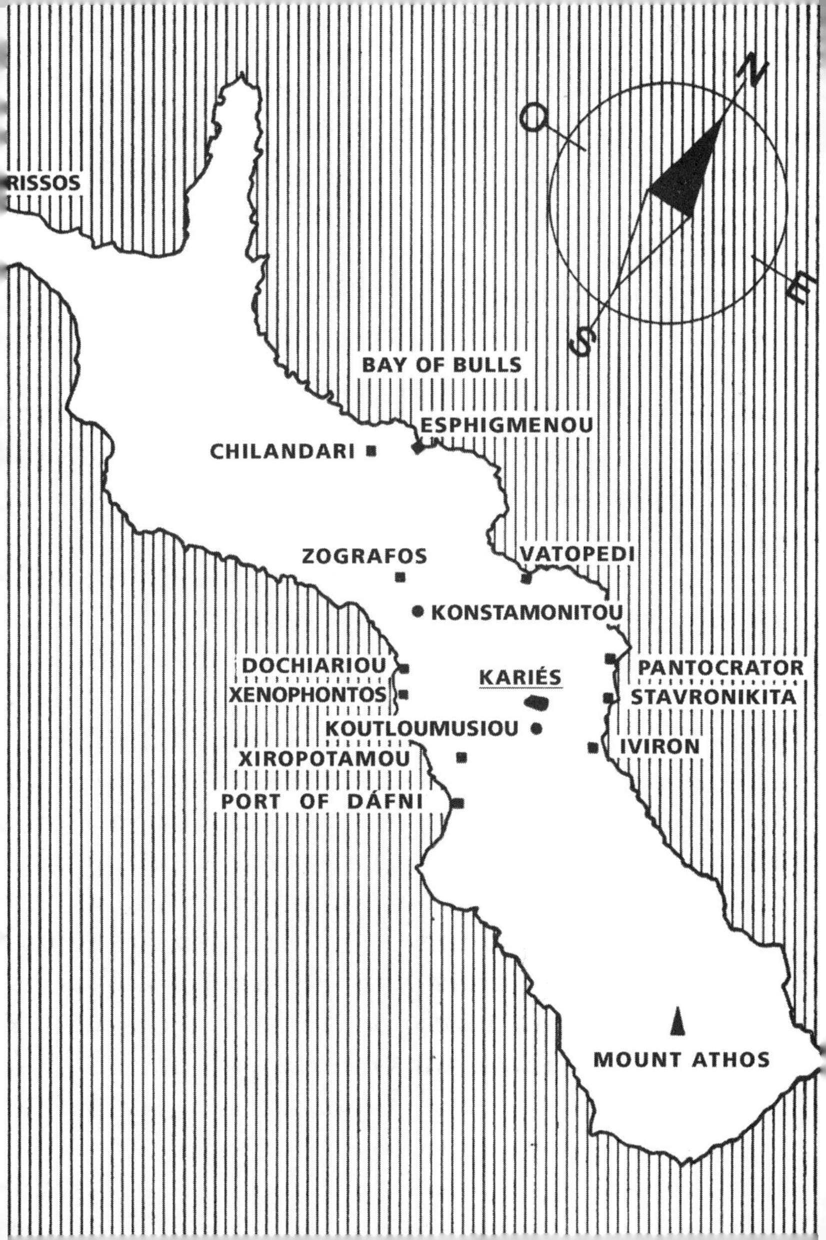
RISSOS
O
N
E
S
BAY OF BULLS
ESPHIGMENOU
CHILANDARI
ZOGRAFOS
VATOPEDI
KONSTAMONITOU
DOCHIARIOU
PANTOCRATOR
KARIÉS
XENOPHONTOS
STAVRONIKITA
KOUTLOUMUSIOU
IVIRON
XIROPOTAMOU
PORT OF DÁFNI
MOUNT ATHOS

Sunrise in Caracalla

Father Athanasius
Monastery of Pantocrator
Mount Athos

To Monsieur Yves-Gérard de La Paumelle
Assistant Director of the Department of Byzantine Paleography at the Bibliothèque Nationale
living on rue de Lübeck, Paris [France]

In the name of Christ, the Virgin and Saint John,

1 February 1965

Sir and most estimable scholar,

Your erudite work in our monasteries, and particularly your most honourable stay at Pantocrator, have left good memories; that is the least one can say. My passable knowledge of your immortal French language gives me the distinguished pleasure of being in a position to write to you, and to remind you that I was of service to you by being your interpreter for a few days for my colleagues who speak only Greek or Serbian.

Possessing your precious Paris address, which you consented to put on a piece of paper for me as I insisted, I am allowing myself to send you a small package, the modest gift of a poor monk. It is only a pound of little fruits, gathered in my garden; holy fruits from Athos! I also send you my blessing.

After this delicate attention, may I consider myself authorised to ask you to send me by return of post, if you would be so kind, and as quickly as possible: three kilos of gunpowder. I need it to manufacture cartridges to kill the wild boars that are laying waste to my estates; it is currently impossible to procure any powder in the grocery shops of Kariés.

I am sure you have not forgotten poor Father Athanasius, the lucky owner of a water-clock that has made him famous on Athos. A clock that you yourself declared admirable after gazing upon it, even though it was not working that day. I hope even more that you remember that I had the honour of contributing to the success of your researches in our library on account of my knowledge of French. In consequence of which, and as a mark of thanks, you will be sure to post me the powder I need with all due speed.

You will find a manuscript under the fruits; I am giving it to you as well, in the hope that you will pay me a fair price for it, if that seems fitting to you, my dear sir.

I knew the author distantly. He was seen when very young on Athos, then when very old, and he disappeared completely after withdrawing into the region of the caves. In his youth he was treated in our monastery following serious burns; later, I tell you again, he left for the upper slopes, and was never seen again. Mule drivers discovered the manuscript this winter at the edge of a precipice, and brought it to me.

I have read this Journey to Mount Athos. *Your fellow-countryman's sole mistake was to believe that there are only stupid folk on the Holy Mountain. The Wise Men hide themselves, do not flaunt their light; and I am one of them. I have my weaknesses, which do not prevent my knowing more than you about the great mysteries. Knowledge that goes back a long time before Christianity persists among us, and is kept secret; it comes to us from ancient Egypt, from the Gnostics and from India. Because of that, this account did not astonish me, this voyage to the Land of the Spirits.*

From a certain level of consciousness onwards, the real and the imaginary, life and death cease to be perceived as contradictory. Was your compatriot dead or was he alive among us? Did he dream his journey on the Holy Mountain? The question is no longer asked once one attains Wisdom.

Whatever it may be, here is the account of a soul preparing itself to see God. In this book, time is not that of human kind. It is ceaselessly changed, broken apart, disjointed, because of the proximity of most holy eternity, which is already clearly felt. For holy souls, a slow DESTRUCTION OF TIME *is exquisitely perceptible from page to page and almost line to line. So, in sending you this text I wish you much pleasure, sir, if your taste is more for the Eternal than for this century.*

That being said, I hold it against our author that he openly mocks my water-clock, which nonetheless required a great deal of work on the part of a skilled workman, and cost me a fortune, so much so that I have remained quite impecunious and almost without money; I must also tell you that I have in my service a young Greek who is dear to me and ruins me. I am penniless. I am therefore counting on you to post to me what I ask of you.

In expectation of the powder, and for the money you owe me for the manuscript enclosed with my package of little fruits, I send you, my dear sir, my religious consideration.

ATHANASIUS

PART ONE

What was the Final Door, and
how did one pass through it?
H P LOVECRAFT
Demons and Marvels

Towards the southern hermitages

I

THE VILLAGE OF WOMEN AND CHILDREN

A GENTLE SURF broke peacefully on the shingle of a very wide bay. Taking advantage of the cooler evening air, young women sat on the wooden stairs that led up to verandas, rocking newborn babies to sleep in their skirts. Not a man was to be seen, not a cry to be heard. Nothing but quiet conversation in the gardens; here and there, songs in a harmonious language. When darkness fell, paraffin lamps were lit. Although I could not quite place this strange land inhabited solely by women, I was sure I had been here before.

Nor was I unknown here. Young girls, in groups of three or four, were walking barefoot on the warm sandy paths in the shade of eucalyptus trees. Some of them gathered round me, and one took me by the hand. We walked among the heavy scents that rose from the gardens and the trees. We headed towards vast areas of shade. Other young girls had got there before us; laughter and jokes rang out: "A boy, a young man!" they cried. "Is this your lover who has come back tonight?" asked the friends of the tall, beautiful girl who had grabbed my hand, whispering in her ear. I was dragged even further into the eucalyptus trees. "Go on, kiss him!" her friends urged. "What are you waiting for?" She took me in her arms and held me close, her friends still surrounding us and watching our every move. She offered me her soft cheeks. I kissed her on the lips.

With more peals of laughter her friends discreetly fled, leaving us alone beneath the low branches of the trees, in what was by now complete darkness. She lay down in the dry grass by the reed hedges. I stretched out beside her, not far from the sea. The water was so quiet that I could scarcely hear the waves breaking.

I questioned her: what was this village where I saw nothing but children, young women and young girls?

She replied that it was called Ierissos, that it belonged to the land of death, and that I was dead. Before returning to life I could stay here for a little while, or continue my journey. I would be very well looked after by her and by her companions. The houses of Ierissos have delightful little bedrooms with whitewashed walls, and beds " … very good for love!" she laughed, and took me in her arms. "I shall make you a fine child!" She was warm, desirable and simple. Long plaits hung over her shoulders; I could feel her broad hips and supple waist beneath my fingers.

"Do other dead people travel further?" I asked.

Our eyes had got used to the dark and I thought I glimpsed sadness on her face.

"Yes, some just pass through. Like you they arrive one evening, and when the night is over they set off for the Holy Mountain. They are taken over there," she went on, pointing towards a sharp peak, a dark mass standing out against the distant horizon of the sea.

I asked her more questions. She did not know the Holy Mountain, for it was forbidden to women and children. But according to the dead men's accounts it was a very wild region, inhabited by monks who followed a strange cult in the worship of even stranger gods. She felt no desire to go there; she was afraid of it, and felt a vague hatred for the place. Every night a boat came across from there, sailed by an old man. Supplies were brought down onto the beach and quickly taken on-board. Without a word the man bought a little bread, some cans of oil, paraffin, cigarettes. Very occasionally travellers got on after buying a few things in Ierissos. The boat sailed away immediately. The village made a modest living from this trade with the Holy Mountain. Did I want to go there?

The moon was rising over the sea, casting a vivid light on the snowy peak of the mountain that was out of bounds to women, making it seem very close across the smooth water. She told me it was not actually snow but spotless white marble. She added that thick forests covered the slopes of this mountain, where bulls wandered freely and spent the winter in caves. The monks, about whom some stories were not fit to repeat, prayed and sang, especially at night, in their peculiar monasteries whose walls were covered with frescoes as old as the world.

I got no more from her. So did I want to set off for the mountain straight away? My questions had seemed so full of curiosity that she was sure I was determined to rush away as soon as the old man's boat arrived. If so I must buy supplies for the journey right now. The little shops of Ierissos were open until midnight; she offered to go with me; reluctantly we stood up. She took me in her arms one last time and gave me her lips. Then and there I almost gave up my decision to go on into the land of the dead. Her whole being smelt of love, tenderness, profound pleasure, unlimited sensual delight. She seemed to have come straight from my dreams: still an adolescent, healthy, naked under her almost childlike white dress that was drawn in at the waist by a light belt. But in the distance, on the motionless sea, shone the bright peak of the Sacred Mountain, which drew me irresistibly towards it.

We went back into Ierissos. In the warm night the young women were still rocking their babies in the doorways; the children were playing on the sandy paths; the peaceful gardens smelt good. We headed for the shops, which were lit with a strange light from paraffin lamps; modest stalls kept by little boys and their young sisters. I bought cigarettes, tins of milk, sugar, snake-bite serum (for I was told the Holy Mountain was infested with them), instant coffee, matches. All of this was put into a sailor's bag which I took in my hand. The night was drawing in; the lights went out in the little houses of Ierissos; it was time to go down to the beach to wait for the old man's boat. Having paid for my goods I suddenly realised my sweet companion had disappeared into the darkness without a goodbye, as if I had been called away never to return. I did not look for her; the children were shutting up shop; I went towards the surf that was tirelessly washing the shingle.

Beside the water a young boy was keeping his eye on some chests and bags of bread. I propped myself up on my elbows in the sand; we waited for the boat. Soon we heard the sound of an engine. A white hull and masts appeared on the deep warm water. The boat's engine cut off and it heaved to in front of us. The old man threw a rope to the child, who wound it round a stake stuck in the shore. He put a plank across the side of the boat and slid it towards the beach, helped by the little boy who had waded thigh-deep into the water. That done, the old man came ashore, loaded the sacks of bread and the chests, lit a storm lantern, took a few banknotes out of his pocket and counted them carefully, then gave them to the child who went away. He put out the lamp. Without a word, without questioning me, he let me climb aboard. He slipped the mooring rope, pulled up the plank, restarted the engine and put it into reverse. The shore disappeared slowly into the night. Once we had gone a little way he turned the helm and headed out to sea.

I sat in the bows, up on the roof of the bridge. A cool wind stroked my hair. Choppy waves lifted our little boat, and it smacked back down again onto the black water. It was the very end of the night. The stars were getting faint and going out one by one. The huge mountain was outlined against a deep blue sky, already bright in the east. The pure white peak, which we were gradually approaching, slipped slowly out of sight behind some enormous hills. I could not take my eyes off it. It shone like a perfect diamond among the last stars that were reflected in the sea.

II

FIRST STEPS ON THE HOLY MOUNTAIN

AT DAYBREAK the white marble peak had disappeared beyond the densely-wooded slopes of the Holy Mountain.

Vast green hills appeared before my wondering eyes, a wide bay, and a long beach. A small fortified castle on an island seemed uninhabited and ruined. The old man steered for the beach. We sailed further into the bay. There, the sea was calmer; large meadows sloped right down to the water's edge. Bulls, the only inhabitants of this tranquil bay, either stood in the shade of beautiful trees, lay on the shingle or came down to dip their muzzles in the early morning foam.

When we were within earshot of the little castle the old man cut the engine, stood up in the stern of the boat and gave a loud shout. No one answered. The domes of a humble chapel were visible above the battlements. Another shout remained unanswered; no one lived on the island any more; the bay was frequented only by black bulls. A wood of cypress trees, probably near a spring, raised their dark heads in the distance. Sparrowhawks soared over the wild bay, a favourite place for herds that were always free.

The engine dead, our boat bobbed on the waves. The sailor called one last time in the silence of the countryside that lay prostrate in the summer heat. A bull bellowed; the cicadas sang.

Starting the engine, we set off again. The Bay of Bulls moved slowly into the distance, and we ran into more rough waves. Our boat plunged through them dangerously; the wind was very strong and the sea was deep. We had to get round another headland and pass close to steep cliffs. The waves were constantly washing across reefs that just broke the surface of the water, giving us no respite. Just a few hundred metres away we saw caves under the sheer drop of the cliffs: black caverns lost to the sun, where the cold green water thundered, laden with white foam; while no great distance from these ocean grottoes that were prey to the tide our boat floated on clear, transparent water.

We rounded the point with the engine at full throttle. Several times I thought we were going to break up on the shallows, which seemed impassable. But each time the old man made use of a strong movement of the waves which lifted our vessel, and managed to negotiate the channels dotted with little islands into which the sea hurled itself with a torrential noise, then withdrew silently, taking most of its water back out to sea. Slack for a moment, the waves resumed their tireless onslaught of the coast. Leaning over the side I often saw the shadow of our boat passing over the clearly visible sea bed, over great blocks of stone that had fallen from the cliffs, rocks submerged since the beginning of the world, for ever motionless under ten metres of water, creating a maze of Cyclopean stones split open by huge fissures where silver fish were swimming.

The uproar of the waves was dying down. We passed one last reef, not without difficulty, and I caught sight of an inlet. The tall façade of an astonishing monastery stood right at the edge of the shingle. Its damp-ravaged walls, pierced with little windows and arrow-slits, reared up in the shadow of the cliffs, facing the sea. It seemed very old, exposed to storms all its life. At that time of the morning the sun lit up only its grey stone roofs. A little jetty stuck out into the sea. The old man called, as he had done before, near the island in the Bay of Bulls. He slowed the engine, passed very close to the silent monastery, then continued his journey on the foaming sea.

Cliffs, sad and black and out of the sun, loomed over us like a gigantic wall. Totally virgin jungle covered the lower slopes of the Holy Mountain. No axe had ever rung out in these woods which, in narrow gorges, came right down to the waves, their flowers and leaves exposed to the spray.

No footprints on the beaches where a thousand storms had hurled piles of pebbles, witnessed by no one. The birds and insects sang fervently in this high jungle. We were so close to it that it almost entirely blocked out the blue sky.

Suddenly I saw the first inhabitant of this land of the dead, a lone man standing on a rock, dressed in a monk's habit gathered in at the waist by a leather belt. His long grey hair was tied in a chignon at the nape of the neck, and he had a white beard. Ageless, a basket in his hands, he waited for our boat. He watched us.

Without moving a muscle, the folds of his black robe blowing in the wind, he saw us try, and fail—because of the waves' continual movement—to hold our position close to the rock for a moment. We threw him the boxes, a sack of bread and a can of oil, which he gathered together in front of him, taking care to step back every time foam sprayed up.

Using the engine, rolling from side to side, we headed out to sea again. A hundred metres above the shore, in the thickest part of the vegetation, I thought I spotted the wooden balcony and plank roof of a hermitage, from which came a thin trail of smoke, like incense offered just to the glory of the birds, the trees and the sky.

Without slackening our speed we passed several monasteries built on the rocks. The coast was still very steep. We went round another headland; the old man turned the helm towards land.

With the engine on slow we entered a bay, and headed for some beautiful meadows where there was a very old monastery with thick fortified walls, wooden balconies and stone roofs. For a few moments I glimpsed the bright peak of the Holy Mountain, then it disappeared again behind the hills. Cutting the engine, floating on clear blue water, silently we came alongside a small jetty. A bird was singing in the forest.

On the shore stood a square tower, along with several other buildings that also had wooden balconies and stone roofs, beyond which I saw old kitchen gardens. A long ramp made of flagstones that had been forced apart over the years rose towards the monastery. Everything looked completely dilapidated, abandoned, known only to the birds and the waves. The tide gently wet the shingle, and a hot sun shone over the meadows.

"Iviron," the old man told me, making it clear that I had to get off.

He leapt onto the jetty and tied the mooring rope to a rusty old ring; he grabbed my bag, and held out his hand to help me to my feet. Then, getting back on board, he slipped the mooring and left me alone on the Holy Mountain, on the first morning of my death.

I was getting used to my new state. I did not know who I was. Apart from that I felt very much alive. The total loss of memory of my past, far from bothering me, gave me a feeling of unconstrained high spirits, lightness, invincible youth, even audacity in this land of the dead with its incredible and savage beauty. Scarcely born into my new life I had only one desire: to venture further into this strange land, which it seemed I was discovering on a June morning because of the bright blue sky, the mass of flowers and the gentle green of the meadows.

On the jetty, bag at my feet, I felt attracted, fascinated, as if I was being watched; as if I was expected in this Land of Souls. The air was fresh and crystal-clear; a thousand flower scents mingled with the rumbling of the sea. The wind from the sea bent the tall green grass of the meadows which lay in the shadow of the old walls of Iviron. The mysterious call was becoming irresistible;

my astonishment at living beyond death was turning into unalloyed joy which I felt with all my new soul.

Slowly I went up the ramp leading to the monastery entrance. I saw stables, abandoned sheds with heavy doors, locked with keys that were lost for ever. A bronze tap filled a pool older than history; the water flowed along stone channels into the gardens; climbing vines, where bees were gathering pollen, shaded a sort of alleyway with paving stones worn down by a hundred generations of mules. Not a sound, except the bees and the water. A cat was watching me from a stable loft.

I walked under a dark archway. I entered the courtyard of Iviron. Wooden staircases, several storeys of balconies, with old beams painted in the same blue as the sky, covered the walls of this vast internal courtyard. Nobody! The cat had followed me. Refusing to believe it was the only inhabitant of Iviron, I chose the first staircase I came to. Accompanied by the cat, going from one storey to the next, from landing to landing, I reached a corridor leading into the depths of the monastery, which smelt of incense and mould. A door opened when I pushed it. I went into a dark little sanctuary decorated with wooden carvings and pictures on gold backgrounds, showing unknown gods and angels, barely lit by a narrow arrowslit which looked out on to the jungle. I closed the door of this inner chapel. The old floors creaked under my feet. Here and there they threatened to break. Other, even darker corridors led only to ancient latrines whose round holes gave a view of lovely kitchen gardens twenty metres below, close to a stream.

I opened another door and went into a kitchen. I might be dead but I was hungry. A hearty appetite, sharpened by the fresh air, made me open the smoke and dirt-blackened cupboards, which were empty except for a piece of bread on a dusty shelf. I took it, sat down on a chest and sank my teeth into the stone-hard crust, almost leaving all my teeth in it. It was the strangest kitchen imaginable. With its enormous frying pans, grills, forks for basting meat, its rotating spits, cauldrons and pans big enough to roast a calf, it owed something to the torture chamber and the forge. Whole trees could easily have fitted into the hearth. Above the sink, which was hollowed out of the wall, a little window with broken panes looked out on to the foaming green sea.

The piece of bread made me hope that Iviron was not just frequented by cats and mice. I was still very hungry; and I was even more impatient and curious to meet the inhabitants of the Holy Mountain: pious anchorites, venerable hermits who were in direct touch with the angels and were filled entirely with contrition. The cat had settled itself on my knees. Exhausted by my sea journey, I fell asleep.

Heavy footsteps in the corridor and the loud, furious sound of boots suddenly made it clear that here, piety went with a dash of vigour. The door was thrown open with a hefty shove. A hairy monk entered the kitchen and planted himself in front of me, hands on hips. Politely I stood up, letting the cat slide down my thighs and hide under a table. I explained to my host that when I arrived … that same morning, starving because of … the sea air, I … had taken … the liberty … of eating … a single piece of bread; without adding that this was only because I had not found anything else in his foul kitchen. He would not listen and reproached me, somewhat awkwardly, for searching through cupboards that did not belong to me. Tired of allowing myself to be treated as ill-mannered, as well as being starving hungry, I made the excuse that since I had only recently died I was not yet familiar with the proper practices in the Land of the Spirits.

"I am dead," I groaned.

"I am dead too," he exclaimed roughly, "but that doesn't prevent me from knowing what delicacy is!" I almost retorted that he handled delicacy the way he opened doors, with his fists. But, thinking it wiser to be conciliatory, and repeating my apologies, I asked him very humbly to give me something to eat.

"Nothing!"

He told me clearly, while stroking the cat, which had reappeared from under the table, that if I wanted to stay in the after-life for a while I must have authorisation from the Great Ancients who ruled over the Holy Mountain. They lived at Kariés, and gave to certain deceased individuals … a parchment allowing them to travel on the Holy Mountain for a few days, a few years, more rarely a few centuries, to knock at the doors of the monasteries, to ask for board and lodging. In short: no parchment, no bread.

Then I shall go to Kariés, I told my furious monk who, to end the conversation, lifted the cat up onto his shoulder and led me on to a wooden balcony from where he showed me a deep, thickly-wooded valley and the tops of distant hills: "Kariés! Kariés!" I asked him to at least tell me how to get there. With bad grace he came down to the fountain where I had left my luggage. From a stable doorway he took a sturdy staff and put it in my hand. He pointed out a mule-track heading into the undergrowth. "Kariés, Kariés!" he shouted one last time, in the voice you use to tell someone to clear off. Then he went back into his monastery, followed by his cat.

The path climbed into the hills and soon almost disappeared in the dried grass. Under the hot sun of the early afternoon the jungle bellowed with a thousand insect cries. Their shrill songs made me numb, my bag weighed on my shoulders, the slope was getting steeper by the minute. In the trickiest places, steps cut into the rock made it possible to negotiate the worst stretches. I had yet to see a snake, but these hills, covered with riotous vegetation, cut through by deep ravines full of dead trees and rotted stumps, must suit them. I stopped: the constant, strident cry of the insects was becoming almost maniacal.

The path now led down into the deepest, densest undergrowth, where having to crawl slowly over dried leaves made me more and more terrified. In places, old paving slabs overrun by vegetation showed this was an ancient path, once easily usable. But several centuries of little use had made it a shadow of its former self. I had long since lost sight of the sea, and pressed on through this fearsome jungle, striking the ground with my stick for fear of meeting snakes. Yet the path on this side of the woods was beginning to return to its original form, that of a firm mule-track. I made good use of it, and walking got easier, my staff rapping loudly on the paving stones in the full heat of the afternoon, made worse by the maddening cry of the cicadas.

Suddenly, at the bottom of a wild gorge I saw a delightful bridge, a stone bridge shaped like a donkey's back, very old and narrow. Peaceful water filled natural pools. I was dripping with sweat, and was drawn to the water. I went down to some long flat rocks, sleeping in the sun in a tangle of dried-up trees left behind by floods. I was washing my face, when to my horror I saw an adder come to the surface and head straight for my lips. I leapt back. On the rocks other adders slowly slithered away into the black water, or into dark parts of the undergrowth. There were angry hissing noises under the branches, and the sound of rustling leaves. These pools, deep in the jungle, in the shadow of the bridge, belonged to the snakes alone.

I moved away, shaking with fright, and resumed my long march to Kariés. The path, now almost visible again, climbed steeply. The noise of the insects was still deafening, the heat overwhelming. I got lost in the undergrowth; the path went no further. There was nothing but jungle as far as the eye could see. All I saw was more slopes and deep valleys, absolutely impassable. I retraced my steps, losing an hour's efforts in the space of a moment. Going back to the Bridge of Snakes, I took another path. Everything seemed mysteriously arranged so you would get lost; it was left to your instinct to decide if a gap in the undergrowth led up towards Kariés; as though this ascent of the first foothills of the Holy Mountain, imposed on all those who wanted to stay here for a time, had no other aim but to discourage the fearful and the weak. My heavy bag, thrown over my shoulder, was dragging on my wrists. My strength was almost exhausted, although I realised that I was often taking paths whose great age was alarming. Some deeply worn step, cut out of the rock, showed that generations of anchorites had trodden on it for a thousand years; an old spell still lingered in these woods. The jungle was beautiful. In its untamed extravagance it might have been laid out by invisible presences. Ruins in the thickest parts of the forest dated back to a time of ancient grandeur long since overcome by the power of the vegetation.

I was nearly at Kariés; my mountain track became a path bordered by walls hiding secret gardens. Many houses with wooden balconies and stone roofs rose in terraces among the cypresses and the vines: a large village. Other mule-tracks joined mine. One last effort; up several steps and I entered a narrow lane, so thirsty I was dreaming of pure, plain water. In the late afternoon everything seemed to be sleeping. Heavy padlocks fastened the doors of tiny shops. The inn was open and I went in, at last finding cool and shade, wooden benches and tables. The landlord brought me *raki*, coffee and water; never had cold water seemed more exquisite, or coffee more delicious.

"Who was I?" my host asked. I did not know. To him this quite simple confession seemed to bode well for my stay in the after-life. I was not one of those dead people who missed the world, who remembered they had been this or that. I was a good dead person, still young, most agreeable, and very attractive: a handsome face, good, good! He rubbed his hands as he devoured me with his eyes. It was enough to make me think I had entered the house of an ogre. I questioned him about the Great Ancients, who I must ask for the parchment that would open all the doors of the Holy Mountain to me.

"They are still asleep at this time of day", he said, and advised me to rest quietly in his inn while waiting for the Great Ancients to finish their siesta.

At five o'clock in the afternoon I headed for their palace in Kariés. A marble staircase led up to it. The heat was still oppressive, so I did not mind the long wait in a quaint little drawing room with heavy wall-hangings and closed shutters for the decision that was to be taken about me. I drank a glass of water set out for me on a delightful pedestal table. People were whispering in a nearby room. Having arrived on the Holy Mountain that same morning, I felt such a desire to stay that there was some anxiety mixed with my pleasure at resting from my exertions in this strange little drawing room, which seemed to date from the last century. I still did not know who I was. Did

I warrant a long stay in the paradise of pious souls? A dignified old man half-opened a door and handed me a parchment covered with writing I could not decipher.

"How long may I stay?"

From his friendly smile I understood that I was allowed to remain for … a considerable time. He led me back to the top of the marble staircase. With a sweeping gesture he showed me the whole of Athos, for that was the name of the strange land which I could henceforth explore as I wished.

Evening came. The narrow streets of Kariés were now bustling. Mules led by young grooms brought heavy loads of fragrant wood from the mountain. Twenty mules entered a courtyard; the loads, unfastened in one handy movement, fell onto the paving and flagstones with a crash. Through the open doors of the shops I saw an incredible assortment of sacks of pepper, paraffin lamps, cans of oil, hooks, rat-traps and ships' rope which attracted the monks from round about and the hermits who had come down from their caves. A cobbler's hammer was striking ancient soles with gusto. I passed my inn; not much wanting to sleep under an ogre's roof, I asked my host if some monastery could offer me lodging.

The monastery of Koutloumousiou was not far away, he said. But I must get there as quickly as possible, for a strict and very old rule stated that the doors of the monasteries must be closed at dusk. He showed me the way. I went down the steep slope of a poorly-paved alley which headed towards a stream singing softly in a little valley. I crossed a bridge. The moon was rising above the forest. Cypress trees half hid the venerable old roofs of Koutloumousiou. Close to the stream the air was cool. Tall black pines smelt good in the calm of the evening. Again I encountered the secrets of the near-invisible paths and the undergrowth, which at that time of day were full of bird-song. A gate opened on to an orchard. I went through it, walking quicker. I arrived just as the door was being securely closed with iron bars and chains. I showed my parchment with its three signatures. I did not know how long it gave me the right to stay among the dead: I was reassured as to the number of days or centuries I had been accorded simply by the respect they showed me the moment I walked in. Clearly it was a length of stay rarely granted.

The door crashed shut behind me. I walked under a cold archway. It was an old monastery, repulsively dirty, its walls green with damp, its wooden staircases on the point of collapse. Rotten planks covered the edge of a well; old vines were dying on wretched old trellises. Some of the walls had once been whitewashed, which only drew attention to the crumbling state of the large stone roofs and the scarlet church that stood in the middle of the courtyard paved with round pink stones. More than twenty cats were congregating outside the kitchen, out of which came a dreadful stench. This was the way I was taken to the refectory.

The last glimmers of daylight lit up long black tables and benches. I sat down with five or six monks who were eating their supper in silence. Most of the tables in the refectory were empty, which was far too big for the last survivors of a large community. A very old monk was eating alone. Another was reading out loud from a text which he chanted slowly in the delightful calm of the June twilight. A small jug of resinous wine was put in front of me, along with a pewter plate of poorly-fried fish floating in a cold rancid sauce, a piece of bread, and cutlery which was also made of pewter and had never been washed.

Black hoods pulled down over their foreheads, crouched over their crusts, the monks took not the slightest notice of me. They were all getting old, with long white beards, skin the colour of ivory; and were poor beyond imagining. I ate my bread discreetly, drinking the whole jug of delicious resinous wine in little gulps, my horrified lips shuddering as they touched the dirty metal. Yet at the same time, the divine peace of the evening, as well as the presence of these very holy old men who I seemed to have known for all eternity, plunged me into a deep joy, a sort of exhilaration. I was back among my own people! Arms bare against the rough boards, feet bare in my sandals, wearing cotton trousers and a shirt torn by the brambles, with all my youthful strength I searched my mind for ancient memories … one evening, among other evenings on the Holy Mountain. On a white wall at the far end of the refectory, a sombre god painted on a heavy panel of gilded wood was looking at me. The scent of flowers from the nearby forests came in through the open windows; cool air caressed my face. I had already lived, I had died several times! This brotherly meal, this poor food, this delicious wine, this savage, handsome god: I had known all of it already! Without attempting to work out when, in which century or in which lives, I gave myself up to the joy of returning. As old as the world, I closed my eyes with happiness: an old man who has died a hundred times, I was young again in paradise.

I was taken to my room through a labyrinth of staircases and dark corridors in the very depths of an abandoned wing of Koutloumousiou. I was left. Such joy had seized hold of me, springing from the certainty of having already lived, and knowing myself to be immortal, that I lay on my bed for a long time, doing nothing but listening to the birds. My narrow window looked out on to the green expanse. Night was taking over the woods, the birds' songs were getting faint. Soon came the great silence of the countryside, asleep under the moon. As far as I could tell my room was in the oldest part of the monastery, where I was completely alone. Not a sound; I opened the door slightly. A lantern lit up a corridor. I went along it and got lost in the darkness. Guided through the shadows by a strong instinct, I found a wooden balcony that opened wide on to an enormous dreamscape of indescribable beauty.

Far below me in the distance, blurred by the darkness into a single ridge-line, the vast forests of the Holy Mountain sloped down to the sea, which sparkled like a bright patch. The perfect disc of the moon shone brilliantly in a clear vivid sky, equalling the cut-glass splendour of the white summit of Athos.

From my blue wooden balcony I could see dark valleys and cypress trees. The moonlight touched mysterious orchards and meadows. I sat down on a bench. Here and there, little bells tinkled in the darkened countryside, which smelt of fresh grass. Left to roam freely outside Koutloumousiou, mules wandered peacefully in the night, shaking their bells, whose faint, metallic tinkling created a strange, crystalline music in the nocturnal fairy-land under the silvery sky.

I was about to go back to my room when loud blows on a piece of wood echoed inside the monastery. Blows that were hurried, then spaced out … Other brief blows in the peace of the night. A persistent call which, when it ended, made me aware of the great silence, even the unfathomable mystery of the tranquil darkness. Footsteps in the corridors. I went down to the courtyard, which at that time of night was like a gloomy water tank, dark and sad, cut off from the moon which only lit up one white wall and one old roof. Lights were being lit in the scarlet church, the colour of old blood. I followed some monks who slipped in through a low door.

For the second time a distant memory made me certain that nothing here was foreign to me. Like them I kissed the lips of a god painted on the browned gold of an icon, and took my place in the stalls where I remained standing, arms on the arm-rests. A ceremony was beginning. Old men untied coils of rope, slowly lowering large silver chandeliers whose lamps were lit using a taper on the end of a pole. With much grating of pulleys, the chandeliers, shining like constellations, rose back towards the vaulted ceiling, bringing out of the darkness frescoes and a hundred icons stacked up in unbelievable disorder. The silver chandeliers, the holy iconostasis, the ancient gold of the icons all reflected the gentle light of the flames. From fresco to fresco, demons and angels fought over souls among the rocks of a dreamlike Sinai. And, against a background of divine darkness haunted by all the stars, they carried on their eternal battle right up to the domes. The floor was marble. The old men crossed the threshold of the most holy iconostasis; they opened a door set with gold and ivory, pushed aside a velvet curtain. A chant as old as the world began in a sad murmur. It grew louder until it became a delirious song to the glory of the martyrs and the gods of the sovereign night: a song of love of an inexpressible beauty; tears, sobs, shouts of joy alternated sweetly, constantly exalting the eternal life, at the heart of the divine light, of adolescents tortured under Nero, under Diocletian, in the times of other gods. The air was heavy with the smell of incense and wax. The voices poured out like exquisitely gentle balm on flesh flayed to death, burnt with red-hot irons, quartered, and which now rested, for ever glorious, in the bosom of Abraham in the innermost heaven. Every night the monks of Koutloumousiou remembered the torments of the martyrs and praised the Lord, Creator God of the stars and the galaxies among all the lights of their fiery church. Novices, with hair long like girls, slept standing up in the stalls. The *Igumenos*—the Abbot—lit a censer decorated with tiny bells, swung it in front of the holy images with a great jingling sound, and walked round the chancel. Everyone in the stalls bowed and breathed in the exquisite perfumes of happy Arabia in a cloud of incense. I lowered my head as he passed in front of me. They kept on singing; their elation kept growing; quickly they carried their sacred books from one place to another, all the while crying out to the glory of God; they lit lamps and put some out. They were in Paradise, creating new stars, snuffing out ancient suns with one breath, singing and running here and there. Then this heavenly festival, which carried on from one night to the next, suddenly ended. The songs stopped. They lowered the great round chandeliers that hung from ropes. The gentle flames of the lamps were blown out one by one. As if at an order from God on the night of the Last Judgement, the stars died. The cold chandeliers, like nebulae extinguished for ever, rose back towards the darkened cupolas. Already several monks were leaving, kissing the lips of their god one last time. Outside, nothing at the heart of the great darkness gave rise to any hope that dawn would soon come, except a delightful silence that heralded the day.

III

CHARMS AND ENCHANTMENTS

I OPENED MY EYES in my little room at Koutloumousiou. The sun was shining in a perfect blue sky. I was young on the Holy Mountain! Free to explore it as I wished. Merrily I went down to the courtyard. The gate was open and I went out. To my right, a path led to the sea.

It sloped down steeply towards long-abandoned *sketes*. An incredibly strong rustic force came from these ruined farmhouses; I walked quickly past. The dilapidated gates now only protected gardens that had long since grown wild. On piles of fallen stones, lizards were warming themselves in the sun. The cicadas sang in the old olive trees. Rampant vines were taking over their trellises. Wooden scythes and pitchforks still stood outside doors that I tried unsuccessfully to force open, such was the fascination I had for these humble dwellings reclaimed by the jungle. On Athos, as soon as you moved away from the monasteries the powerful vegetation covered everything. These deserted farms, some of them with cupolas of flat stones housing a shrine, now belonged only to the buzzing bees, the lizards and the snakes.

Athos: Holy Mountain or Paradise of snakes? Or both? Suddenly, in the shade of a fig tree, I saw a grass-snake that was so long it must have been a hundred years old. Given its age, it was in a way as venerable as the Great Ancients who ruled in Kariés. A member of the species known as the Esculapius grass-snake, it was a good three metres long, and lay motionless beside a pool, watching me. Was this the father of all the snakes on Athos? I thought I saw in him the great primordial serpent. He did not run away, or attack. Had his skin, shed a hundred times and renewed each summer, also attained wisdom? But a different kind of wisdom? He was handsome. His black and green scales shone in the shade of the tree. His forked tongue ceaselessly flicking in and out, he slowly uncoiled and disappeared among the lower branches.

My path went on, always downwards. In the long green grass it became a sort of street lined with *sketes*—the homes of peasants without wives. An open door: I entered a room with a red brick floor. There was a rusty anvil, a cart-wheel, a broken-down bed, rakes, a barrel, a straw hat. I took it without a qualm. A forgotten icon rotted against a wall. More than God, the great primordial serpent now haunted these dead houses that smelt violently of hay, whose powerful scent spoke of coarse sensual pleasures, themselves also very ancient, of solitary gardeners and young shepherds. I was wild with heat, fear, curiosity. I re-emerged, hat in hand. Thirst tormented me in the blazing sun. I saw a well beside a trellis overrun by hornets, an iron bucket on the side, a rope; and I noticed my face reflected in the calm water of this deep well. Who was I in this wilderness where everything kept reminding me that it was not unfamiliar? Had I already drunk this delicious, icy water? Had I rutted in these stables when the galleys of Byzantium were sailing off Athos? The sea sparkled in the distance … fragments of my distant past were coming back to me. I put off remembering them until later and set off again, using steps cut into the rock, heading towards the unchanging sea, wearing a fine straw hat, bare-chested, shirt thrown over one shoulder and my stick in my hand.

My road ended at the Bridge of Snakes. Iviron was not much further. I arrived in the middle of the afternoon, and my first concern was to drink at the little fountain. I went into the courtyard, feeling almost at home: was it not here that I had come ashore on the first morning of my death? Yesterday: already it seemed that a far greater time than one day separated me from it! The church was open, and singing was coming from inside.

I went in, tired and exhausted, blinded by the sun, terrified by the snakes, happy to rest in the shade of the painted arches. Monks, barely woken from their siesta, were singing vespers. Not much wishing to show myself, I walked in the passageways and dark chambers around the chancel. The gold of the icons shone gently in half-darkness. Far from the blazing sun and the Jungle of Snakes, I felt at ease in these mysterious little rooms of God, furnished with old stalls, and where the stagnant air smelt of incense and grime. Silver lamps burnt continually in front of the holy images. There were wooden panels, heavy and gilded, varnished, soft to the fingertips, delightful to the lips, showing the Son of God, the Virgin, and John the Baptist. The flames of the lamps, that in places had blackened and eaten away at the paint, but respected the unchanging gold, made these venerable pieces of wood very similar to the burnt, tortured flesh of the martyrs. In these chambers of Spirits inhabited by all the gods of the heavens, in these storehouses of souls, in these consulting rooms of prayer, frescoes showed the Battle of the Angels against the Great Serpent: clapped in irons in the deep cavern of an impossible desert made up of bizarrely drawn rocks, it escaped for a thousand years before being conquered. It was as if all these efforts to show the faces of the gods were nothing more than an immense fairytale invented by people who, like me, were terrorized by the fear of snakes.

At the end of Vespers, racked with hunger, I went to the kitchens. With the idea of getting a reasonable meal, I show my parchment to the monk who had treated me so badly the morning I arrived. He snaps at me that his fires are out, he frightens his cat with his shouting, declares that he has nothing and, in conclusion, asks me to follow him to the cellar. We go into the storerooms. There are bundles of firewood, heaps of logs, barrels. He gives me plenty to drink. In the darkness he feels my arms, fingers me, cuddles me, pinches me, finds me to his taste. This great famished man imagines he is devouring me. According to him I have delicious flesh. Soon he is pressing me against him. His black robe smells of cheap wine and grime. His beard prickles me. When he is sated from the mere thought of eating me raw, he locks the cellar and goes about his business.

My hunger appeased by the resinous wine and the caresses with which I had been favoured, I sat down on a bench in a corner of the great courtyard of Iviron.

From here I saw the immaculate peak of Athos, clear and white above the green forests. In a sky that was still blue, the bright moon rose beyond the battlements; it sailed peacefully across a clear space. The fresh, gentle air of the June dusk touched my face. I was young on the Holy Mountain, delighted by everything, very free: to go from one monastery to another satisfied a strong liking for wandering which came back to me from a distant past which it seemed I was reliving. I was totally happy in the calm of the evening, filled with forest scents.

Suddenly, a sort of call rang out in the depths of my soul, which I knew was very old; a silent call. I was seized by the idea that I had a master on Athos. I had known him for all eternity. He was calling me! I had already lived on the Holy Mountain. He knew I was back. He wanted to see me again. Where did he live? In which monastery, in which *skete* of the Jungle of Snakes? The call, for a moment incredibly strong, fell silent, leaving me to myself and to the decision to go in search of my ancient master. I would have set off immediately if the gate of Iviron had not slammed shut, showing me it was now too late to wander the paths.

Instead it was time to beg for lodging and supper, as the resinous wine I had drunk in the cellar and the pleasure of being caressed had only appeased my hunger for a moment. I climbed wooden staircases, went from floor to floor until I was right underneath the old stone roofs, again delighted with this unfettered life, this perpetual wandering which suited me so well. At the sound of my footsteps in the corridor someone opened a door. A monk, seeing I was hungry, invited me into his room. From a kitchen cupboard he took a pan full of black beans which he put on a table. A paraffin lamp was burning feebly there; he trimmed the flame and stood in front of me without a word, but with a sort of profound kindness dating from the first evenings of the world. I watched him while I ate my beans: an old man, very tall, his hair and beard the colour of snow, his hands long and pale; a man who was slightly absent. When I finished eating he took me to a distant room and returned to his own.

Whitewashed, its only furniture was a metal bed. A window with heavy iron bars opened on to the countryside. I was in no hurry to sleep. I propped myself up on my elbows on the sheets, which were intensely white in the light of the moon. The window, cut deep into the thick walls, did not look out on the seaward side but on to the gardens, and forests so vast that they half-hid the clear sky. Beautiful moonbeams lit up the kitchen gardens of Iviron, the pools, the trellises, stakes supporting peas, low walls made of grey stone. Unseen birds mingled their cries with the murmuring of the tide: for a moment they were quiet in the woods, and the sea gave hints of its presence with a peaceful sound of water. Then, taking up an age-old dialogue, in the peace of the night the calls of the night creatures answered the slow breaking of the waves. With incredible clearness the silver light sketched out the dark hills, the old gardens, the leaves, the black cypress trees of this Land of the Dead. The thought of being called, most likely never to leave again, filled me with boundless joy. I closed my eyes with delight, opened them again, still amazed to see the unmoving, wild magnificence of the Holy Mountain, asleep in the bright moonlight. Knowing I was in Paradise brought me perfect happiness. Who was I? I suspected that my total loss of identity was the necessary condition of a long stay beyond the gates of death. So I accepted wholeheartedly that I would be nothing but a gaze, a soul full of wonder at the sight of the gardens and forests of Athos on a moonlit night, among other clear nights on the Holy Mountain. I had dragged my bed up against the window: bathed in moonlight, lying half-naked on my white sheets, a stranger to myself, I fell joyfully asleep.

The decision to go and search for my ancient master got me out of bed in the morning. The monk who had taken me to my room gave me some bread and a bottle of water. I did not forget my fine straw hat, my staff, or my bag of simple provisions for the journey. Thus equipped, I went down to the sea at first light.

Next to a square tower dating from Byzantine times, several monks dressed in black robes, their hair tied-up into chignons, were mowing some grassy meadows and making haystacks not far from the vast, incredibly lively waves. The air was fresh, the thunder of the surf unceasing. In a hurry to find my master, I left my hosts to their idyllic haymaking and went north along the shore. Sandals in my hand, feet soaked by the foam, I walked along the shingle, which was constantly threatened by sudden mad rushes of water which washed the beach.

Rocks that would have been dangerous to walk on forced me to take a path that climbed into the hills, but it kept close to the sea, which I glimpsed through the indentations in the coast. The sea air blew very hard here; bees were buzzing in the blue sky, gathering pollen among the bushes and a field of yellow flowers, in which I disappeared up to my waist. The path soon came down to a beach that was sheltered from the wind; my footsteps crunched on the shingle of a tranquil bay. Not a wall, not a *skete* in sight. No tracks except my own across the unmarked sand.

Each day I got more accustomed to my new life. With no other memory except the certainty that I had already lived, I was born to absolute existence. This primordial state summoned up every desire and sensual pleasure—stripping naked, I walked into the sea, full of the joy of being young. I cooled my face in the waves, which were shallow at this spot. Clear water lapped over the virgin white shingle. I had picked some flowers and strewed them round me: they floated, bobbing gently on a slight swell. Facing the distant horizon, wearing only my straw hat, I washed my manhood in the cold water among the flowers, my hips, my beautiful naked thighs caressed by the ebb and flow of a gentle tide. In this state of nature I became more susceptible to the beauty of the world: a hot sun shone on this bay of earthly Paradise; the birds were singing in the undergrowth, the bees were buzzing;

the shore formed a perfect arc, mirrored by the lovely curve of an enormous hill, so green under the blue June sky. For a moment I had thought I was completely alone. On this morning of my new life was I alone with the power and might of the vegetation, the clear water, the birds, the bees, all of these simple reflections of God, just like me? I went further into the sea, lost my footing and let myself sink into the transparent water. With slow strokes I swam down to very fine sand where light shadows danced. The sea bed fell away quickly; far from the bright surface, great rocks guarded the entrance of a wonderful sapphire-blue valley. I brushed against seaweed and sad caves; with the merest movement I went lower. I soared over silent abysses … Man or nymph or soul, was I now no more than a glance? Multicoloured fish came within arm's reach. The water, whose blue was getting darker and darker, was now almost black, and it frightened me. In a gentle glide I rose slowly back towards the light, towards the constantly-shattering mirror of the sunlit waves.

Back on the sand I fetched my stick and my clothes; I left the tranquil bay behind me. I walked along by the sea with no other care than to satisfy, as soon as possible, the hearty appetite that last night's dish of beans had barely appeased.

I was soon in sight of a monastery on a steep headland. It had the distinct look of a fortified castle, with its square towers and wooden balconies clinging to walls overhanging the sea. Mule-drivers I met along the way told me the monastery was called Stavronikita, and that it was poor, which seemed to augur badly for the way starving travellers would be treated.

Contrary to this unkind assumption, a monk, stepping aside respectfully for me, asks me to come up to the boudoir. At the top of the monastery is a charming little drawing room, rather Turkish with its divans, its cushions, all very ethereal, suspended in mid-air forty metres above the waves that roar against the rocks. On three sides of this delightful room, twenty small windows give a view of the blue and green water and the vast horizon. One window is open: he closes it immediately for fear I may be bothered by the strong wind from the open sea. He gets me to sit down on a divan … completely at my ease; he slides a cushion behind my back, disappears, comes back with a silver tray, on it a small cup of coffee, a large glass of water and a plate containing a finger of jam. He places it all on a round table in the middle of the drawing room. I want to get up, approach the table. But I must stay on the cushions, rest from my fatigue. He puts the tray next to me on the divan. A forgotten teaspoon obliges him to disappear again. Here he is, back again, with a delightful little spoon which he sinks into that finger's length of exquisite fruit preserve. My coffee is not too sweet? I find it to my taste. He is reassured. Is my water too cool? It suits me well. He smiles with pleasure. He is at my disposal: I mention that I have not eaten. At these words he runs to his kitchen, comes back with a lace cloth which he throws on the table; he sets out knives and forks, all silver; he brings a carafe of water and asks me to consent to wait a moment. The moment becomes an hour: forty metres below me the sea is crashing; the little windows shake in the gusts of wind. At last the door opens: he appears, plate in hand. He brings up a chair and I sit down at the table in front of a small white cheese and a crust of bread. That is all; there is nothing more to hope for; better to leave! A boat seems to be wanting to drop anchor at the foot of Stavronikita. I thank my host and run down to the shore, just in time to climb aboard.

At the helm was the old man from Ierissos. He asked me if I wanted to return to life. I told him I preferred to stay on Athos, that I was in search of Wisdom and a master. He offered to leave me at Pantocrator, which was in sight. I agreed, and we headed towards a harbour hollowed out of the rocks in the shadow of several Byzantine towers.

He gave me onions and wine. Long green swells coming in from the open sea caught the boat sideways on, lifted it up, passed under the hull in a slow movement before going off into the distance to smash themselves on the reefs and the beaches. It was early afternoon and the sea was strong and beautiful; the sun warmed the wooden hull; our heavy little boat sunk into deep foaming valleys that were strangely silent. Then, with a great surge from the engine, sputtering on the clear water, it climbed back up the slopes of the untiring sea. Pantocrator was approaching. We made slow headway, rolling on the stormy sea, deep and cold. We were hit by new breakers that hid the horizon for a moment: the vast horizon, lost then found again each time the waves passed.

The thunder of the surf echoed against the rocks that were now no more than a cable's length away. We had to pass through some narrows. Our caique, its engine on slow, rolled at the foot of the high walls. We took advantage of a lull in the waves to enter the channel. A heavy swell came in; it lifted us up stern first and threw us into the harbour with a cascade of spray. Engine idling, we fetched up gently against a quay built of large strong stones.

There were fisheries with wooden balconies supported by crude, roughly hewn beams, older than the first crusades. Some ancient boats, pulled up onto dry land, had almost rotted away. The old man unloaded some wooden chests then put out to sea again. At the entrance to the channel, a fisherman was casting his line into the eternal tide. In the distance, the blue foothills of the Holy Mountain stood out against the horizon of the sea.

I walked up to Pantocrator. I went into the courtyard, then the church. I had a rest by the icons. Monks were getting ready to sing vespers in the cool shadows of their church. To me it seemed all the more silent and peaceful because I had come from the uproar of the water, which still echoed in my ears. My eyes seared by heat, light and salt, I was almost blind in the presence of the holy images. The memory of the bright green sea was still in the depths of my aching eyes, and superimposed itself on the faces of the gods painted on heavy pieces of wood: Christ, the Virgin, the great green waves! The perpetual tide, the angels, the gold of the great wooden panels! For me, arriving from the sea, these icons had the look of primitively-painted flotsam, scarlet, midnight blue, ochre and black, colours of the after-life.

I was drunk with fatigue and thirst. But the sweetness and strength of the old Byzantine chants which now rose under the domes gave me a delightful rest from my worries. Sad and solemn chants, suddenly deliriously happy, then sad again. There was a motion in them like the tide: from far away, from an eternal ocean, they gradually rose up to take my soul by storm, broke up like spray into shouts of joy, tears, and washed away my tiredness. Then they seemed to withdraw. It was now no more than a murmur. Slackening off for a moment they came back, tireless, like great rolling waves. Glorifying the Lord, the bearded monks answered each other from stall to stall. Their church was full of treasures from distant expeditions to the Divine. From them they had brought back Christ, the Virgin, the saints, copper candlesticks, silver chandeliers, a shining iconostasis, painted images. At the end of vespers, when they had congratulated each other on their pillaging, when they had spent a long time scenting their treasures, their wrecks and their gods with incense, they left the church and disappeared into the depths of the monastery.

I went out into the courtyard and drank water from a fountain. At Pantocrator, none of the monks seemed to be my master. I wanted to reach Esphigmenou before nightfall. In the kitchens I was told it was impossible. Esphigmenou was more than a day's walk away. Better to hope that a caique would come by. Waiting, hoping, arming oneself with patience: that seemed to be the prevailing law on Athos. Good luck was on my side. A boat saw my signals and quickly took me aboard at the entrance to the harbour.

Long shadows were already stretching out over the sea and the dense forests of black cedars that covered the slopes of the Holy Mountain. The boat was piloted by a young fisherman, almost a child. We were travelling fast across the water, which was now calmer. Without slackening our pace we passed Vatopedi, and an hour later we saw the inlet, beyond which stood the sad monastery of Esphigmenou. Clad in grey stone, worn away by damp, forever cut off from the sun, its tall façade rose up beside the water, lashed for centuries by the waves of the great winter storms, which seemed to have broken several windows. Under the latrines, which were recognisable by their narrow openings and the long trails of black filth that stained the walls like a sort of leprosy, the smell of rotten fish, dead seaweed and excrement hung in the air.

The child slept here every night. We landed at a small jetty. He took loaves and fish from a chest, and a jar of wine, and we went down to the shore, making the shingle crunch beneath our feet. A cold surf washed along this mournful creek. We climbed a slope paved with little stones taken from the sea since time immemorial, we went under an ancient arch; a poor rusty lantern lit up a painted Virgin at the back of a niche rotted by the spray. Esphigmenou seemed in a state of dilapidation that was verging on the dire; so I was very surprised to see the inner courtyard with its many arcades cheerfully painted white, a fountain of bright marble, pretty vines with ripening grapes, in unexpected contrast to the grim façade that faced the sea. In a tower, chimes sounded. Then, in the calm golden air of evening, came the clear sound of a heavy blow on an unseen bell.

The clock's one hand showed a time in the afternoon, or the night. But I knew that on Athos, time is not that of humankind. The sun was setting beyond the hills that I glimpsed above the roofs. The child suggested that I have supper with him. I followed him; a second door opened on to the countryside. He lived outside the walls in a little mule-driver's house near a pond; a half-ruined house of unspeakable squalor where he lit a fire in a narrow grate. I sat down on some wooden bed-boards covered with a sort of litter made of torn cloths and straw. He slept there, apparently not suffering from the poverty in this little house with glassless windows, and walls of dried earth which were lit by the first flames of a fire of vine shoots. He set the fish to fry in a pan, added hot peppers and salt, which he took from the bottom of dirty little boxes containing fish-hooks, thread, needles and lead weights. He gave me some delicious resinous wine. This encampment, this insouciance, this mess pleased me in the sweetness of evening. In this poor house, black with smoke and filth, everything was witness to a strange joy of living which gradually took hold of me. The child slept on the boards. He put his humble treasures in little tins; he owned a boat. He was very happy: that could be seen from his measured, solemn movements, his reserved smile, his joy in welcoming me. He had found happiness in the Land of the Dead. Now he was making coffee. This strange house, inhabited by a child, seemed to date from a far-distant time when young sailors went to sea alone. This touched me personally, as if I had once been this child. At the very least, might I have known him in the past? Was Mount Athos not an incredible storehouse of memories and dreams? Like me, did some dead men come back here to sleep occasionally? The resinous wine, a charm as old as the world, gradually made me drunk. I was falling asleep in front of the fire, on the clothes thrown on the wooden bed-boards where I was thoroughly happy, right down to the distant depths of my wild, affectionate nature. He had ground the coffee in a funny little cylinder with a crank handle, the water was boiling, night was falling. The child stretched out affectionately beside me and held me tight: he wanted me to stay with him tonight, and other nights, for ever! I would have agreed to resume a life I had already lived a few centuries before; I would have been a sailor with him on his boat again, and been satisfied with that dream among so many others, had the monks of Athos not exercised a more powerful attraction over me. For I had been a monk in an ancient time, that I remembered as night fell. I must go back to the monastery! I gently kissed his hot lips, his beautiful eyes. I left him quickly, for the outer door was being closed, while at the same time the sound of chains echoed from over by the second door, which opened on to the sea.

The chimes sounded the third hour of the night. It was time for me to beg my food from door to door in the shadows. I went up to the first floor and into very dark corridors whose cedar-wood ceilings smelt of mould and the forest. By the light of a small lantern I glimpsed strange, gilded wood-carvings; I noticed a chink of light coming from under a door. I went in. A poor paraffin lamp lit up some ovens. I asked for bread. A monk gestured to me to sit down and wait a moment. In the warm glow of the lamp, among the shadows thrown against a wall, he stirred up the hot coals and soon put in front of me a bowl of soup which I drank without a word, my elbows resting on the dirty wood of a massive table, telling myself once again that it was my destiny to eternally beg for soup at monasteries in the early part of each night. From a window there was a view of the black hills of the Holy Mountain, the lamp was slowly dying, close to the ovens an icon glowed. An ancient happiness made me linger in this kitchen, with its overpowering smell of ingrained filth, rancid oil and strong spice. My hunger subdued, I was sure I had drunk soup a hundred times in this kitchen at Esphigmenou. Here I am, back again, I thought. To be caught up in this maze of time for who knows how long, to find myself back in this monastery, young again, very free, made me more drunk with pleasure than the tot of *raki* I had just been given. The monk wanted to padlock the door of his kitchen before going to bed; I had to leave. But who was I, from one life to another? Who stood up, thanked him for his kindness, kissed his hand? Who was it who was taken to the door of a distant bedroom? And who fell asleep, drunk with joy?

And who was woken up, and by whom, around midnight? The monk who had given me soup was sitting on the edge of my bed. He took a dried fig out of his pocket and slipped it furtively into my hands. He was a fat man burdened by his belly and by his luxuriant beard. Sitting on my sheets as he was, his short legs did not touch the floor, so this religious man found himself in a most awkward position for keeping me company. Breathing heavily, he settled himself more comfortably on my bed, and in the darkness he sought out my face with the tips of his fingers like a blind man. Delicately he pulled away the shirt that covered my shoulders; with a lecherous moan he threw himself on my bared flesh; he sank his sharply pointed teeth into it, growling like a beast and pinching my hips. Caught unawares by this visit, I had propped myself up on my elbows on my little bolster so as to be better able to face up to this great outburst of appetite. My host was crushing me with all his weight; I knelt on the bed and, more comfortable in that position, let my famished friend do as he wished, accustomed as I was to the sudden insatiable desires of the good monks of Athos. He devoured my shoulder for a little while, then murmured sweet nothings to me, afraid he might be caught in the act of devouring a young traveller in the middle of the night. His robes smelt of filth and old cooking pots, his rough beard scratched the little opening to my ear. Then suddenly he stopped whispering that I was desirable and listened closely in the darkness. Reassured by the silent corridors, he set to devouring my shoulder again, still growling with pleasure, and pinching my hips so hard that I moaned with pain, which seemed to sharpen his taste for fresh flesh. The iron bed groaned under the weight of my host, time passed slowly. I saw that one of the white walls of my bedroom was lit up by the moon, and leant one hand against it. The narrow window looked out on to the cold, gloomy inlet where I had come ashore; a powerful smell of dead seaweed rose from the near-silent sea in the depth of the night. From my bedroom under the old stone roof, more than fifteen metres above the quiet water, I heard our boat, lifted up by a slight swell, bumping now and then against the stone slabs of the little jetty. I ate the fig. I was moved by my host, I felt pity for him. He trembled with pleasure as he devoured me! I was very hungry as well, but I could not throw myself on people. To me this old man seemed very childlike; I had the feeling of being older than him, wiser, as old as the world despite my adolescent appearance. My young body housed an old soul, very human, capable of compassion, of great tenderness, of kindliness: kneeling on the edge of my bed, I lowered my eyes. He was on the point of proving his virility to me, seducing me as one might a girl, when footsteps in the corridor filled him with alarm. They went away, but it had ruined his appetite. He tried to revive his hunger by pinching the nape of my neck with his sturdy fingers, but his heart was no longer in it. He was very upset, and cursed the unwelcome visitor who had spoilt his pleasure. No more appetite, no more joy! My discreet efforts to restore my host to a state in which he might finish his supper met only doleful indifference. No longer hungry, he soon gave up the urge to dine. Furious with himself and with the weight of years, he got off my bed and readjusted his clothes. He kissed my cheek; by way of a compliment he gave me one last pinch, so hard that I would have cried out in pain, had I not had the best sort of nature you could hope to find in a boy you wake up in the middle of the night, eat raw and use as if he were a girl. He half-opened my door and crept off into the darkness. My entire body painful, exhausted, my soul happy, I fell asleep again, rocked by the sound of the waves breaking peacefully on the shingle in the little creek. Two or three times I heard our boat drag on its moorings then drift back to shore, bumping gently against the jetty: four times perhaps, no more; for I sank delightfully into heavenly sleep.

Did I wake in a cool cavern at the bottom of the sea? Cold, blue-green, iridescent, murky, the colour of unsettled water, the beautiful light of morning was reflected by the mirror of the waves. It danced on the ceiling, on my bed, on the whitewashed walls of my room, which faced north, away from the sun, and so remained in sad, tranquil shadow. Gentle waves ran over my face and hands.

The metal bars protecting my window made the shape of a cross against the horizon. The window embrasure was cut so deep into the thick walls that I could sit in it as if it were a sort of lodge. With the coming of day the wind had got stronger; powerful breakers crashed over the rocks and ran into calm pools that they whitened with foam. The sea shone pure emerald under a bright blue sky. While I was asleep the caique had been moved away from the jetty, and was firmly anchored a few ropes' length from the shore, rolling heavily on the waves. There was no question of travelling by sea today. Best continue my journey on the paths that led deep into the countryside. Yet there was no hurry to leave Esphigmenou; the kitchen must be closed at this time of day. So I stayed at the window, face pressed against the bars, never tiring of the sight of cold waves attacking the coast.

Was it being near the water that made me prone to metamorphoses? My strange night, the aching muscles that were the result of it? This land without women led you to femininity! On Athos, through lack of food, through want, you were only too liable to stray into delicious errors and, because of solitude, to find everything within yourself. Like Adam in the first days of Eden, with Eve inside him, part of his flesh, I suspected there was a wife inside me. My host's caresses had dragged her from her peaceful sleep: she wanted to live, to see the world, to walk about! I wanted to be a pretty girl, if only for a few days. On Athos, near to the Divine, in a land where no two clocks showed the same time, nothing seemed ridiculous. Accepting the feminine part of my character in a vast uncertain time would be an unbounded joy! The sea rumbled against the rocks, the wind slapped me in the face. Esphigmenou's chimes sounded the fifteenth hour of the morning … This strange temptation melted slowly away. Soon all that was left was a feeling of slight surprise and a much greater desire to know more about this Holy Mountain, where everything happened as if by magic.

In a corridor, under a lantern that was still lit, a thin trickle of water ran from a brass tap into a stone wash-basin. I filled a metal jug and went back to my room. I had sugar and powdered coffee in my luggage. Going back to the deep window frame I made myself a sort of cold collation, which I drank quietly while watching the waves at play. Then I shut the door of my room without a sound and went down to the courtyard without meeting anyone. I went out through the gardens; for, because of the storm, I wanted to go through the woods.

A well-paved path led towards the shore, running through kitchen gardens, past vines and little stone walls before rising into the hills. The battlemented towers of Esphigmenou sheltered it from the wind. At a sudden bend I saw the sea again, which was hurling its green waves against the shore. I was deafened by the sound of the shingle constantly rolling around in the surf, and the thunder of the waves breaking on the rocks. The caique danced on its anchor ropes; and, on that side of the gardens, the wind off the sea shook the brightly-coloured leaves of the olive trees.

A stream ran out of the forest, its shallow water meandering down to the first flecks of foam by the sea. A small stone bridge straddled across it. I leant on the solid Byzantine stonework of the wall and watched the peaceful water, the green grass: at the sight of my shadow, at the sound of my footsteps, twenty fresh-water turtles left the bank, dived down and plunged deep into the mud where they immediately disappeared.

Leaving the surf and the Turtles' Bridge I headed for the high ground overlooking the inlet. The path became a track, passing farms whose doors had been closed for centuries. By the time I saw beautiful meadows at the edge of a wood, I had long forgotten the restless sea and the noise of the wind. Inland, a hot sun burnt above the motionless countryside. Black bulls wandered in a valley. Bare-chested, wearing my straw hat, my blue shirt thrown over one shoulder, I strolled into the tall green grass; gingerly I went as far as the olive trees, where I stopped by meadows that had never been mown, and where the bulls came past. I had a rest in the shade of a tree, one hand against its rough bark. My eternal soul quivered with happiness at the sight of so much peaceful beauty. I was free on Athos! Happy to the depths of my being! Again I sensed that a woman, a woman within me, and for me alone, shared my joy of living! Who was I? Completely myself at last.

How sweet and charming was the feminine part of my nature, which I was now discovering! Always ready to roam the countryside, cheerful, knowing me from all eternity, always willing to give me pleasure: tender and faithful wife, I would have held you tightly to my heart, I would have had you, right there at the foot of the tree, if I had not known that we were one single being!

She was still very young, an adolescent, and the bulls frightened her. She wanted to go on into the long grass; we made a wide detour to avoid the black bulls that were moving closer to the forests in the growing heat. Some of them noticed us and raised their heads. We hurried to safety across heavy stones lying in a stream.

There were lovely trees, shade and cool grass. She was afraid of snakes. Taking a reed I whipped at the thickets and grass, and we made a clean sweep of the place. I stretched out beside the stream with my young wife; I shut my eyes and went to sleep.

When I opened them again a bird of prey was soaring in the blue sky of Athos. I picked up my staff and headed further into the green pasture. The long grass hid old wells: in the past, generations of wise gardeners had ploughed this peaceful valley. I often came across abandoned *sketes*, low, crumbling walls, orchards overgrown with brambles, age-old vines where snakes slept, cherry trees that had gone back to their wild state. Ancient wooden bridges meant you could still cross the streams; densely-tangled copses filled with bird-song covered the slopes of the Holy Mountain. Its wings outstretched in the azure of the morning sky, a buzzard flew high up a long way off, over this tranquil, beautiful place which, since the last hermit left, had been almost divine. Once heavily populated, Athos was reverting to jungle. Perhaps, imperceptibly and from century to century, from season to season, from day to day, it was returning to the hands of God.

A path seemed to lead past the Bay of Bulls, which I had glimpsed on the first morning of my death. From the brisker air I realised how close the sea was. The black bulls I had seen near the forest were the very same ones who had been cooling their feet in the gentle white foam on the morning I arrived on Athos.

Bells tinkled, and there was the sound of hoofs approaching. Travelling monks, mounted on strong mules with novices riding behind, blocked my path in an olive grove. Seeing me, the monks yanked on the reins and stopped their mounts. The mules pawed the ground, whipped their sweating flanks with their tails as the horseflies attacked ... I barely had time to put my shirt on, so as not to be caught half-naked.

Who was I? Was I going to Chilandari? They had just come from there. I answered their questions as best I could—questions which were asked, what is more, in an extremely rough manner: I was dead, as dead as dead could be; I assured them it was so! Did they want to see the parchment I had been given by the Great Ancients of Kariés? I reached into my pocket for it; they told me I could leave it there.

They were old monks sitting on bad wooden saddles, ill-fitting and made softer for their pious posteriors by little cushions. To be more comfortable, each kept the skirts of his robe hitched up, tying the ends to his leather belt with dear little knots. Most of them had a young monk riding on the cropper, who had one arm around the older one's waist while with the other he shaded him from the heat of the sun with a black umbrella, opened out like a parasol. The saddles were overloaded with leather bags, jars of wine, goatskin water bottles, saucepans tied to the pommel, and bundles of old books held firmly between strong wooden boards securely tied up with string. I asked the reason for this upheaval.

The none-too-polite reply came from high in the saddle. They were going to see friends. A fifteen-year-old novice, as lovely as an angel, was kind enough to explain that they were going to spend a week or so with holy men, on condition that they return the favour. In short, people invited themselves from one monastery to another. They spent a good week with friends who, in return, came to see them for at least a week. They went for walks, made the most of the fine weather: pretexts for pious conversations, interesting meetings, theological debates, he added, lowering his eyes like a real little saint. At which, as it was clear I was delaying venerable travellers eager to discuss the twofold nature of Jesus with old friends from neighbouring monasteries; and as the mules, harassed by the horseflies, were bucking, pawing the ground and shaking themselves, threatening to unseat the holy travellers, they set off again with hefty blows from the stirrup-leathers, leaving behind them not so much an odour of sanctity as a powerful smell of urine, sweat and mule dung.

When the travellers had gone I left the olive grove and headed for Chilandari, simply following the tracks left in the dust by the mules' hoofs. There was no risk of getting lost, since the path was clearly visible through the middle of the fields, which at this time of day had been deserted by the bulls.

A tall square red-brick tower appeared, alone in the middle of the fields. It overlooked the distant sea. I passed this old Byzantine tower and headed into a narrow valley. As I went, my path became increasingly like a proper well-paved road which, with every step, closely followed the dried-up bed of a broad stream running down from the mountains. The best road in Athos!

At the entrance to a cypress wood, a fountain offered thirsty travellers fresh water, which spouted continually out of a bronze tap into a long stone trough. I cooled my face and my hands. The heat was becoming more than harsh. Leaving the road I went into the cypress wood.

It was an exquisitely cool place, full of mystery, shade and peace. Enormous tree trunks, more than a hundred years old, rose high in the air towards distant black foliage which protected me from the sun. Soft grass grew round the base of the scarlet trunks; it was gentle on my ankles, which were tired after the long walk. It was almost cold in here. The air smelt of resin and pine. A thousand pillars of scented wood! A strange silence. Almost darkness, not a single bird-song. A track led on further between the trunks, which went on endlessly into the distance. The grass that got greener, and the delicious shadows, drew me even deeper into this wood of old cypress trees. The damp grass suggested there was a spring nearby; I looked, and found it at the heart of this divinely peaceful wood. A bird—just one—was drinking the clear water that sprang from the ground: the only bird in this temple of trees. It did not fly away. Perched on a stone, it watched me. The birds of Athos do not fear the dead! I was dead, in Paradise, and was aware of the fact. So why should I inspire fear in this bird who was as dead as I was? Did it see me, or was I, in its eyes, merely a soul, a simple presence from which it had nothing to fear? I was beginning to love this bird! Had I known it on the other side of life? Was it a friend, a lover of forests who had turned himself into a bird to live in the woods? It flew away, letting out a kind of call, and disappeared into the top of a cypress tree. I stayed beside the spring for a long time, hoping it would return; then slowly I left the dark clump of trees.

Once again I saw the path leading to Chilandari, whose roofs I soon spotted above the greenery. Walls enclosing orchards appeared in every direction, benches, lovely arbours, old pleasure-gardens where no one had picnicked since the end of the last century.

Chilandari. A large fortified village, almost a town. A hundred roofs of flat stones or tiles covered ancient walls set out in total disorder. Bastions, battlements; several storeys of dilapidated balconies; a thousand windows with small panes; arrow-slits; countless chimneys; the whole dominated by a tall, formidable tower.

The heavy gate of Chilandari stood open, wide-open to anyone who wished to enter, and was approached via an awning supported by blue columns. I went through the first doorway I came to and down a dark passage paved with round stones worn down by mules' hoofs. A lantern hung from the ceiling. Beyond this entrance hall, decorated with a fresco of the Virgin, was a narrow, dark alley-way, hollowed out of the thickness of the fortifications. Along it were tiny shops, carefully padlocked, with shutters, with wooden doors of old workmanship, peculiar, forgotten. A sewer ran past; at the sound of my footsteps, rats scrambled up the walls and onto the roof. Then came a second arched entrance, and I was in the courtyard.

An enormous lone yew tree; a scarlet church with domes. Piles of logs beside a well. I went over to the church, hoping to find shade and rest there. The door was well and truly locked. What about the kitchen doors? They were locked too! Was Chilandari uninhabited? With so many double-locked doors I feared it was. Yet the great door I came through as I arrived from the woods stood wide-open … Chilandari must have been abandoned. Everything had been locked! No, people were wary, that was all! It was mid-afternoon and my head was spinning with heat and tiredness; thirst tormented me. The cicadas sang.

Climbing several steps I reached a gallery just opposite the church which gave me shelter. A bench made of planks was somewhere to sit down along by the side wall. The gallery was separated from the courtyard by heavy stone columns and arcades painted red. The ceiling was of finely carved wood; fantastic frescoes decorated the walls, the whole Apocalypse on the background of a starless night: the foul beasts emerging from the well of abominations, the insects of the last day, with the faces of women, long legs like grasshoppers and scorpion tails ending in a double spike, the saints, Christ, the demons and the angels fighting a final battle under a rain of fire, while the cities of the merchants crumbled and the great whore seduced half of humanity. The cicadas … fell silent, then began to sing again; an angel proclaimed that blessed are they who die in the peace of the Lord. Horrifying demons tortured for ever the adorers of the Beast; an earthquake, a hailstorm destroyed Babylon. Christ, a two-edged sword in his teeth, was treading down the vat of God's anger; a young seraphim carrying a scythe cried out that it was time to gather in the harvest of the elect.

Loud blows on a piece of wood echoed round the courtyard; blows struck one after the other on a sort of beam, then gently, insistently … Silence; the sporadic noise of the cicadas.

A monk appeared with a heavy bunch of keys in his hand, followed by three others. Quickly they pulled down their black hoods, covering their heads, and hurried towards the church, whose door opened with a great sound of keys in locks. Soon, in this enormous monastery which housed only four monks, while the cicadas sang in the forests, the sweet name of God came from the darkened chancel and, repeated a hundred times, rose up to the blue summer sky. The last monks of Chilandari, so solitary and poor they were scarcely more than old jungle gardeners, loved God! They cried out the name of Christ! They adored Christ, called upon Him!

I went into their church. Christ have mercy on us, Christ have mercy on us! Christ the King, Pantocrator, have mercy on us! Glory to Thee, Son of God! Standing in the stalls, leaning on the arm-rests, they glorified the Son of the Lord. They saw me standing humbly in a dark corner; the oldest beckoned me to take my place beside him. I took a few steps, knelt on the many-coloured marble flagstones, got up, kissed the icons of the most holy iconostasis and stood in an empty stall. I was drunk with fatigue, thirst and heat. Blinded by the sun, I slowly got used to the semi-darkness of the church. The wall paintings I saw among the shadows showed the birth of Christ, the baptism of Christ; faint little flames lit up mosaics, Saint Michael speared the Great Primordial Serpent with his lance. High up in the vaulting, angels played the lyre; the prophets and the evangelists, reed pens in their hands, wrote down on long parchments this vast adventure of the spirit, among so many other adventures of God which were unknown on Athos. The bearded monks took books from racks behind the stalls and opened them at a place marked with a bookmark; and, in almost sing-song voices, with bizarre vocal inflections, strongly accentuating certain syllables, one by one they named all the saints, witnesses of Christ, witnesses of the world beyond:

Athanasius, Pachomius, Dimitrius, Vladimir, Boris,
Panteleimon, Gregorius, Chrysostom, Nicholas,
Hilarion, Simeon, Johannes, Basil, Palamas, Philotheus

… and others besides; an incantation that brought back distant memories. An aged monk swung a censer in front of the iconostasis, bowing to Christ, the Virgin and John the Baptist. Then he walked round the church. The censer, decorated with little bells, jingled in the half-light where the gold of the mysterious icons was shining. Each painted board was entitled to its ration of incense. Sometimes he went into the distant side chapels, where the sound of bells became indistinct, and much fainter. You might have thought it was a small horse dying. Then the little bells began to tinkle again, and the monk returned to the chancel. He passed in front of us and I breathed in the sweet perfume of the incense, the delicious fumes. The sound of bells stopped and the censer was put back behind the iconostasis. The lamps were snuffed out and the monks left, placing a final kiss on the eyes and lips of the beautiful face of the Son of the Lord.

I went outside. Everyone was heading off in their own direction without a word, in a hurry to get back to their respective rooms. It was obvious that they cordially detested one another. For years they had been living together, and could no longer stand one another. They had come to a tacit agreement to avoid each other as much as possible.

A monk closed the door of the church, picked up the bag I had left in the courtyard and set off up a large staircase. Climbing from landing to landing we came to a most pleasant drawing room, furnished in the style of the last century. I often got the feeling that Athos was nothing more than an immense repository of wrecks, of fragments of lives and dreams haphazardly accumulated in a place unknown to time and space. A paraffin lamp of complicated baroque workmanship with a porcelain shade hung over a round table covered with a lace cloth. The ceiling was of varnished wood; lush plants blossomed by wide windows. I saw chairs lined up along a wall hung with pale, well-framed lithographs showing holy patriarchs and several characters with full moustaches, fiery eyes and daggers and pistols in their belts; whose existence in the world of men must also date from the beginning of the last century.

One lithograph showed a man who was still very young, and of an almost feminine beauty. This one had no moustache, he was as pretty as a picture. An unbuttoned collar revealed his girlish throat; a dagger, two scimitars, a powder-horn and four pistols had been slipped through the woollen belt that was tied tightly round his slender waist.

As I had stopped to look at this extravagant fellow, my host put down my bag in a corner of the drawing room, and approached.

"Lord Byron," he cried, "Lord Byron, liberator of the Greeks!"

This meant nothing to me. He was most disappointed:

"Missolonghi, Missolonghi," he thought it a good idea to add.

I went up to the lithograph and managed to read: *Byron, 1788–1824*. I tried to remember the world of men. My almost total lack of memory did not weigh heavily on me, far from it. But I was distressed at aggravating my host: my supper was at stake.

"Lord Byron," he shouted in my ear, pointing at the handsome young man. Weary of my stubborn silence, he turned and looked me up and down: I had no dagger at my waist! I was dressed in a blue shirt torn by brambles and cotton trousers; on my feet were espadrilles, and I was holding an old straw hat. Did something in my face suddenly remind him of something he liked about Lord Byron? He softened again and asked me who I was. I replied that I had no idea. I was dead, which was why I begged him to forgive me for forgetting the history of the world, as well as my name.

My frankness and my agreeable manner finally won his respect. He was tall, very old, very thin; kindly, he asked me to sit down, to wait a moment. He soon came back with coffee and *raki*; we sat down at the table. He took a packet of cigarettes from his pocket, offered me one, and we chatted. According to him, dead folk … they were often seen on Athos; but a dead man as dead as I was … rarely! He congratulated me on being so very deceased! The first time you hear this compliment you find it rather embarrassing. Dead people, he went on, we get fifty or so every year! They stay a few days, miss the world, haven't forgotten anything, want to go away again, and indeed do so with the excuse that people on this side of life suffer too much from hunger. I belonged to a different sort of dead person! The real dead: those who have even forgotten their own name during that century, those who are visibly happy on Athos, who stay there for a long time, months, years … He made a sweeping gesture. We drank a second glass of *raki*; he lit a cigarette.

"I would like to see the parchment you were given at Kariés."

I took it out of my pocket; he examined it and handed it back.

I admitted that I had not managed to decipher a single line of this famous parchment.

"No doubt it is better that way", he said, getting up and putting the glasses on a tray. "It is not useful to know the length of time one will remain on the Holy Mountain."

"That is written on the parchment?"

"It is written."

"How many days, months, years, am I going to stay on Athos?"

Without answering, he picked up my bag, led me to my room and threw the bag onto a bed.

I persisted: "Years, centuries? … "

"Or more!"

And he closed the door.

I sat down on the window sill and pressed my young face against the metal bars. It was nearly evening. The birds were calling in the woods. Was I happy or sad? The state of being dead was a very strange one. I thought I had got used to it, but I had not, or at least not much. For the first few days it was as if I was enjoying the surprise of still being alive, as well as my great delight, my joy at seeing the beauty of Athos. The knowledge that nothing here was unknown to me added to my cheerful amazement. The pleasure of seeing the Most Holy Mountain again, so many lovely things, the water, the mystery of the forests, my freedom, my wanderings, had, as it were, distracted me. To hear myself now say that I was dead, very dead, perhaps for ever dead, increased my alarm at having passed into the Land of the Spirits. I was a real dead person! Not one of those who, having walked on Athos for a little while, quickly sail away again after having only glimpsed the Divine. It had not exactly been concealed from me that I was called never to return to the world. I had an impression of great departure, this time with no return. Without sadness. I had even forgotten my name: so who, I thought, as I stood at the window pressing my lips against the iron bars, watching the first stars light up in the bright sky of early night, who—faced with the idea of being dead—would have mourned the death of whom?

Someone knocked at my door. I opened it. It was my host, a white cook's apron tied round him, which made the old man appear even taller, even thinner in the darkness of the corridor. He asked me to kindly follow him. We went into the drawing room; he opened a double door and stepped back to let me enter the dining room, where a place had been set out for me at the far end of a long oval table covered with a spotless cloth. A paraffin lamp, of the same style as the one in the drawing room, gently lit up an earthenware soup tureen, a carafe of wine, a wine glass, a basket of bread, fresh fruit and, on a large silver salver, several vegetable and fish dishes that looked most appetizing. A napkin lay on my plate, folded in the shape of a heart. He asked me to sit down and turned up the wick of the lamp, making the flame give me proper light. Once the brightness made it easier for me to see these marvels and my perfectly-arranged place setting, he opened the soup tureen, delicately picked up a ladle, and served me.

Having got out of the habit of eating I hardly touched this exquisite broth. The old man stood behind my chair, eager to anticipate my wishes; he poured me wine and broke my bread for me. Dreamy at the sight of this hearty supper which I had so little expected, my stomach completely unreceptive, I studied my surroundings. Despite the efforts of the lamp the room was still full of shadows. I could just make out heavy drapes, green plants in copper pots. On the wall, a large lithograph of Moses saved from the Nile by the friendly slaves of Pharaoh's daughter slipped back into darkness as soon as the wick became black. The good monk trimmed it almost constantly, leaning over the food to do so. Nothing was right! That evening, for the first time since my arrival on Athos, I knew I would never return from the Land of the Spirits! I had to get used to being just a soul. I was devoid of memories; and that made me feel lightened. Without regrets, for I remained what I was before: intact and powerful within me, I rediscovered tastes, inclinations, abilities, virtues and vices that I knew were mine. I had lost nothing of my deepest being, I was young beyond the gates of death! Nothing really clouded my delight at the thought of living eternally in the Land of the Spirits, where I felt very much alive, very determined to take advantage of my new state and give free rein to my true nature, which had been slowly assembled through thousands of existences. It mattered little to me that I had forgotten a recent identity. What was my true self, ancient, as old as the world? What was I in the eyes of the Lord? What would to happen to me in this Land of Souls?

My appetite was coming back; so, putting off the process of knowing myself better until later, I tackled my supper. It was high time; the lamp was growing dim. Fried fish, lentils, beans, courgettes, green beans livened up with raisins, lemon, sweet peppers and black olives, everything was hurried. Having finished the wine, I left the table a little drunk, thanking the old man for his unhoped-for good supper. But on Athos, did each new moment not bring a new surprise! He took me back to my room. In the doorway, did he guess that my slight intoxication hid feelings of great confusion? He took me in his arms, held me to him very tightly. He seized my face in his bony hands, kissed me on the eyes tenderly, as one kisses a child. He opened my door and then left, wishing me goodnight.

I stretched out fully dressed on the bed, where almost immediately I fell into a wonderful sleep. In its depths I quickly recovered my strength, lying flat on my stomach, moving no more than a tree stump, my head buried in my little bolster. Strange night: how long had I been awake? The moon was hidden by the hills, and so my room remained in peaceful shadows. What had dragged me from my exquisite sleep at about two in the morning? For, listening to the delightful silence, it must have been the middle of the night. Suddenly I heard hammer-blows on the piece of wood called *Simandron*, summoning the monks to the divine office. Had I heard them before they echoed in the darkness? Or was it simply that a distant atavism, as well as my becoming so quickly accustomed to the ways of Athos, made me wake of my own accord in time for matins? After several short blows, the monk producing them moved along the galleries; the bang of the hammer was repeated here and there in Chilandari, then stopped. Again the heavenly silence of night returned, as tranquil as calm water, like a motionless lake of peace within the walls of the monastery. Should I go down to the church? I had an incredible desire to go back to sleep as soon as possible. So I stayed in bed; I heard footsteps on the stairs, then, ringing clearly on the paving of the courtyard, a door opening, liturgical chants. Where were the toilets? My good monk, all too readily convinced of my spiritual progress, had forgotten to tell me. If I groped my way through the corridors and the dark staircases in search of distant latrines, I might break my neck! I waited until the service was actually under way. Once I was certain that all the monks were praying in church, I got up; and, standing on my window sill, holding on to the metal bars with one hand, I pissed into the courtyard from the fourth floor. It made a marvellous waterfall sound, plashing on the paving stones. Then I went back to bed and fell asleep again. Later on I was jolted from my sweet sleep by the thump of the church door banging shut, by the sound of a lock turning, and the footsteps of people in a hurry to get back to their sheets.

A faint glow shone on to the roof and the great square tower that loomed over everything. The moon was rising, the night was moving on. Suddenly, howling groans, sobs which soon became appalling moans made my hair stand on end! Lamentations of immense sadness. Seized by indescribable panic, I did not move from my bed. Cries of rage; tears that never seemed to end. A concert of howling, yapping, barking seemed to be coming from the forest. Persistent howling, very close, just outside the walls; moans and sobs that made my blood run cold. Appalling, desperate cries; inhuman laments! Several packs of jackals were running and howling in the undergrowth, unwilling to move away from our battlemented walls.

I went to the window. In the moon's cold gleam I could make out old roofs of flat stones, covered in moss, half-green, covering ancient buildings topped by small octagonal domes, strange little chimneys and tiny, triangular skylights. The monastery of Chilandari backed up against the first foothills of the Holy Mountain—steep, impassable slopes. The jungle began just beyond the roofs, the jungle with its thousands of leaves glowing under the clear night sky, the jungle with its dense thickets where these cries came from. The jackals were squabbling over the filth at the foot of our walls. They were fighting under the latrines, carrying away excrement into the woods, devouring it savagely with howls and sobs. The screams fell silent, then began again even louder. The abominable beasts of the night continued their din: one band, pursued by another, climbed very high into the undergrowth. A fearsome dispute made the pitch of the barking get higher. Furious galloping in the copses; crying, yapping! The two packs met in a ravine for a final settling of scores, which outdid all the rest in its unspeakable horror. Then the abominable beasts of the night dispersed, and there was silence.

A nightingale sang. Invisible in the deepest part of the greenery, it called delightfully in the now peaceful forest. It alone was awake beneath the branches, and sang an exquisitely measured song into the clear space. The round moon shone above the hills; its brilliance lit up each leaf in the jungle, I caught the scent of resin and sap. Now peace had returned to the woods, I was about to go back to bed in my little room, which was no more than an attic cubby-hole under the stone roof, when my door slowly opened, then more and more until a shadow appeared.

It approached me. A strong smell of grime came with it. When the shadow was two feet from the window where I was still on watch, I saw it was one of the monks I had barely noticed in the church. Hairy and dirty, he did not look like the good monk who had done his best to welcome me. This one came from the tribe of the filthy and the simple who lived on the other side of Chilandari. Through what maze of unknown passages, by what detours in this enormous monastery had he discreetly arrived at my room? I could not quite see his face, which bristled with grey hair; two gleaming eyes stared at me intensely. Without a word he grabbed me by the waist, tore me away from the window sill and threw me on the bed. Dispensing with my clothes, I promptly gave him every hope for the pleasure he wanted to have with me. He had only glimpsed me in church. Had he guessed from the mere sight of my pleasant, open face that I would not offer any resistance to rustic behaviour? Had I, in the chancel, with my straw hat in my hand, looked like a young goatherd who could not be frightened by old ways? He had watched me all through vespers. Convinced he would not be disappointed, he had come soundlessly to my room and expected from me the sweet, hot submission that gives an attacker the illusion of uncommon virility. Yet in the presence of such alacrity he was speechless. My haste to unbutton my clothes, to offer no obstacle to any effrontery! His senses, worn out by age, did not respond so quickly. Weapon in hand, he hesitated to come and join me; a rusty old weapon, still held so low that it scarcely menaced the naked young flesh offered up to his desires. Kneeling on the sheets, I waited for him in the shadows, away from the moonlight that came into the room. His brutality in throwing a boy onto a bed, without a word, without a caress, came from the days of his youth. His hesitation now came from the weight of years. He sat down at the bed-head; with the tips of his fingers he touched my face. Betrayed by his great age, brushing young eyes, fresh lips, could he hope for other joys? A strong odour of filth came from his person. But the sophistication of the Byzantine liturgy, which had become second nature to him, as well as a long habit of gestures that please boys, and girls, for perhaps he had been married in this same century, gave a strange delicacy to this old gardener's advances. His hand wandered over my face. He sometimes showed extraordinary skill in the innocent pleasure he took in following the curve of my forehead with his finger. When he entered my room he thought he was going to have me immediately, as one rapes a girl. Still well-built, but having overestimated his own strength, he had to make do with kissing my eyes. As for me, completely open as I was to great outrages, I had to be satisfied with the delicious contact of his tongue on my closed eyelids. Time passed. We were at the same point. At last he dared caress my back! Not that he really enjoyed it. But in the hope that his former strength might return, he let one hand drift towards my backside, just in case. With various movements of the other he helped nature regain its lost vitality. The night was cold; the nightingale was singing in the forest; I heard the distant sound of the sea. I was half-naked; my skin, made highly sensitive by the cool air, shivered with pleasure at the first bold caresses. Now he was touching my hips, more and more tenderly, in an exquisitely skilful way. He had already stopped polishing weapons that were no longer unresponsive. With a sudden movement he slid the unbuttoned clothes that still covered my thighs down to my ankles and climbed onto the bed. My long wait, my great impatience, a rather rough assault, soon led to pleasures which, although crude, were no less delicious for that. A night-bird cried; a magic spell came out of the trees: seduced, possessed, taken by violence, inhabited by another, I was no longer alone within myself. In a perfect frenzy, the feminine side of my nature was sharing the eternity of life. I felt myself violently distracted from a solitude that often weighed on me. A shadow draped in black, like an enormous bat that had come down from the dark trees, covered me and seized my body right down to its depths. He had hoped for gentle submission from me. He had come to my little room in the hope that my pleasant face was a sign of artless instincts in love. He was not disappointed! By grunts and furtive kisses he showed me all his contentment. He whispered a thousand thanks in my ear for having granted him more than an hour of my time without the slightest impatience, whispered that his great age did not make him the liveliest of lovers. I was an angel of sweetness and kindness to him! A little pearl! In fact I had that taste for submission, that hint of the slave, which, once all obstacles were overcome, brought his pleasure to heights of pride; and mine to a pure, absolute and simple delight in abandoning myself without hesitation to a strong embrace. He got off the bed, adjusted his black robes, buckled his leather belt, rearranged a few folds. He opened a cupboard, took out a blanket, threw it over my legs, tucked me in gently, placed a last kiss on my forehead like a blessing, and went away, leaving me crushed with pleasure, drunk with joy, delirious. The shadow went soundlessly away down the corridors, back to the mystery of the night whence it came.

Intoxicated with sensual pleasure, moved to my very eternal soul, I was again certain that I had already lived!

Were not ancient customs for me just a trial of magic powers, a call to lost memories? Fragments of previous lives were coming back to me. How could I be in any doubt? I was as old as the world! Swift glimmers of light crossed the shadowy depths of my happy drunkenness. I had been a novice in Russia and the friend of an old monk. I saw a wilderness, an old man and an Arab boy. Had I been the old man or the boy? Or both at once? And in what period? I was a soul in the Land of the Spirits, still able to remember a few images, but had lost contact with the worldly circumstances of how I acquired them. Other recollections that emerged from the darkness of time undoubtedly belonged to me as well. Trembling with emotion and curiosity, in my little bed under the stone roof I seemed to hold the golden key to ancient memories. I saw myself, a half-naked girl prostitute, at the entrance to a cave; as a woman I was gathering herbs on a moonlit night in a wild forest. A sorceress, I had seduced men. Before Sumer, before history! And what was Sumer? Again I saw my depths and my share of shadows. The spell faded. A certainty was still rising up from my depths: I had been a wise man. The illuminated part of my nature was still unknown to me, just as all I knew of the Holy Mountain were its beaches and its lower slopes. I must travel to the snowy regions, to the peace of the summits, to find my true master.

It was as if my excellent host had disappeared. No morning coffee on a silver tray awaited me in the drawing room. So well-treated the evening before, I was surprised by this negligence. Had my good monk forgotten me? Several times during the night he must have crept up to the door of my room to check I was sleeping piously. From the moans from my bed he had guessed I had given myself up to lust; from the whispering, that one of his colleagues was visiting me rather late. Furious, upset, perhaps jealous, he had discreetly withdrawn, leaving me to coarse pleasures. His disappearance into the depths of Chilandari this morning was the mark of his disapproval. The absence of coffee was a reflection of my unworthiness. From now on I would be ignored. There was nothing for me to do but leave. And to convince me, as if that were necessary, he took me for a lout: the portrait of his dear Lord Byron, that distinguished, handsome young man, had been taken down … I no longer deserved to see the liberator of the Greeks! Rejoicing at this ridiculous notion, I went down cheerfully to the courtyard, through the postern gate, and out to look at the gardens.

Immediately on my left, a low stone wall overlooked some stables and pretty vegetable plots. At the bottom of a valley a line of poplars followed the course of a stream that flowed down from the densely wooded, rich green hills that surrounded us. Eagles soared overhead. A young cat, which was playing on the flagstones, rubbed itself against my legs. Liking nothing so much as little black cats, I took it in my arms. Mule-drivers passed by. I touched its backbone. It purred with pleasure; for with cats, unlike boys, there is no dishonour in wanting caresses. Suddenly leaving my arms, it leapt gracefully onto a roof, ventured onto some rickety vine trellises, almost fell into the bunches of grapes, maddened some bees, and slid down a pole. A staircase led to a little house built up against the stables; a cat-flap seemed familiar to it, and it slipped through and disappeared. But two green eyes were soon watching me closely from the opening.

Knowing that on Athos there are only spells, calls and enchantments, I also headed for the little white-painted house. I pushed open a wooden gate. A steep ramp, paved with round stones, led down to old stables whose door stood wide-open, I could see a long line of mangers leading away towards mysterious piles of hay. Once, a hundred mules had been housed here. At that moment, two unsaddled animals, tied to iron rings and attacked by horseflies, were pawing the ground with their hoofs. A violent smell of dung, urine, sweat and straw mingled with the scent of leather from whips, tethers, stirrup-leathers and reins, bound together in bundles on hooks securely fastened to the walls. It would have put the most virtuous of archangels in heat.

I went up the steps and knocked at the door. It was opened: it was a bar. A narrow whitewashed room, a few tables, some chairs; a stove in one corner. Three mule-drivers were drinking *raki*, talking about it in low voices, as is only right and proper when you are a mule-driver on the Holy Mountain. The mule-drivers of Athos: a collection of thieves, widowers and deceived husbands; all of them rabble and good company. I had met more than one of them at bends in the road. Wearing old caps and ragged clothes, in espadrilles or barefoot, poor as Job, and good men by the way, they went into the forests with their beasts to look for wood. They repaired roofs; more often they wandered idly, their only occupation playing discreetly with their manhood through a hole in a trouser pocket. I was given a warm welcome and asked to stay for a while. One of them, half-innkeeper, half mule-driver, put a metal pot on the stove. With its long iron handle he could hold it on of the glowing coals. An exquisite smell of boiling coffee spread through the room. I was offered *raki* and cigarettes. Soon I was given delicious coffee. The cat jumped onto my lap and, charmingly, butted me gently in the face. People wanted to know who I was. I didn't know. I was studied: with my features, my bearing, I could only be German! More than me they had held on to the memory of the present century, and had some idea of their own identity. The innkeeper was a widower, another was just an old thief and didn't hide the fact. That is how I found out, by chatting with them, that it was June in the year 1954, that they were Greeks, and that they hired out mules.

I told them about my plan to go up the mountain. I questioned them at length, for their knowledge of the paths could be invaluable to me. What roads, what routes through the jungle must I take to reach the bright marble peak that could just be seen beyond the hills? My question surprised them. They could not give me any useful information. They did not like my insistence. None of them had been up to the high slopes, nor had they seen the immaculate block of stone from close up. They only knew the lower forests, from which they brought back loads of scented wood for the kitchen stoves. To a man they advised me not to attempt the climb. Just beyond a builder's yard, where one of them had once spent all summer cutting beams, were mysterious cedar woods about which it was best to say nothing. Saintly hermits lived right up high on the mountain; they were not unaware of this, but they had never felt the desire to meet any of them. The summit of Athos: these simple people preferred not to talk about it. They respected it as having been a holy place from time immemorial—holy even before Christ, before the Virgin—without wanting to go there. It was none of their business. And anyway, the jungle was dangerous. The night before, jackals had dared to come right into our gardens. Bulls wandered in the woods, spent the winter in caves and, driven mad by the rut, attacked passers-by. There were wild boars, snakes and deer everywhere. It was best not to move away from the sea. But since I would not budge in my resolve to reach the block of bright marble, one of the mule-drivers stood up and took a coloured map of Athos down from the wall. Pushing aside the glasses, he spread it out on the table.

Athos: a peninsula about sixty kilometres long and bizarrely shaped. I had gone much too far north. I had to come back towards Kariés, towards the south. Beyond Koutloumousiou and the Great Lavra, paths led off into the mountains. They advised me to get to the west coast quickly, via Zografos and Konstamonitou. I asked them to make me a present of the map, which they gladly did.

They reminded me that they hired out mules: did I have any money on me? My pockets were empty; they were disappointed.

More coffee was served. Tired of my questions about the bright marble peak, they went back to their usual talk with pleasure. Several glasses of *raki* loosened tongues that were only waiting to speak. According to the mule-drivers, the monks were nothing but old layabouts who offloaded all the hard work on to them; hoarse old billy goats, completely broken, completely crippled, and singing out of key; greybeards and old misers. The sudden arrival of a young, sixteen-year-old mule-driver, who walked into the inn without knocking, as though it were his home, silenced the tongues. The adolescent had a twenty-drachma note in his hand, and wanted two bottles of oil. He threw the note on the table, took the bottles he was handed respectfully, and went away … closing the door behind him with a skilful flick of the heel. The mule-drivers finished their *raki*. We were about to take our leave of each other. They were warning me one last time about the danger of venturing too high on my own into the forest, when the adolescent came back and asked me courteously to follow him. This time he was holding a hundred-drachma note. He bought bread, *raki*, courgettes and cucumbers. While the innkeeper was counting out his change, the youth, with a gentle hand, lovingly stroked the cat, which was purring with sensual pleasure under the table. He put the coins in his pocket, gave the animal a final caress and a heavenly smile. We went out together, our arms laden with delicious provisions.

We went back into Chilandari. Straight away, we took a dilapidated spiral staircase which led us up beneath the roof. This part of the monastery was the oldest, and the most dirty. At the sound of our footsteps a door opened at the far end of a corridor. And who did I see? My guest from the night before! He came towards us, hugged me, relieved me of the courgettes and the cucumbers which I was holding to my heart, and which excessive demonstrations of friendship threatened to crush; and everyone knows that a crushed cucumber is of no use on the Holy Mountain! He asked me to come into his room, where two places had been laid on a very wobbly pedestal table. He introduced me to the adolescent: his name was Gregorio. He drew water, acted as cook, swept the floor and fetched the groceries. "Having spotted you at the inn with the mule-drivers," he told me immediately "I sent the child back, instructing him to tell you I would be very honoured to receive you at my modest table."

This fine phrase over with, the poor man, not knowing what else to say, showed me his 'apartment', while the said Gregorio danced from one foot to the other, avoiding my gaze. The apartment consisted of only one room. It was furnished with a divan, a cane chair, a mat where Gregorio slept, a chest with numerous locks, an armchair upholstered in yellow velvet and the pedestal table where our knives and forks were set out. Above a narrow window with its broken panes replaced by sheets of oiled paper, stood a paraffin heater on a small wooden plank, along with a bundle of books, a copper bed-warmer and a recent icon showing a pink, insipid Saint George elegantly piercing a friendly dragon with his lance.

A wooden balcony covered with old boards served as a kitchen, and had a view of the countryside where the cicadas sang. Cucumbers and empty bottles were arranged neatly along the edge of this charming balcony, decorated with carnations which grew as best they could in rusty tin cans. A blackbird was whistling in a cage hanging from a beam. Gregorio blew vigorously on the coals of a cast-iron brazier, where three eggs were sizzling in oil in a heavy frying pan. A bracket above his head was used to haul up heavy loads: wood, my host told me, indicating a pile of logs and a little hearth which I had not seen in the semi-darkness of the room.

We sat down to eat. The eggs were fresh, the lentil broth quite reasonable. Clearly I was going from one surprise to another, and was not wrong to believe in enchantments. The evening before, an air of virtue and a passing resemblance to Lord Byron had earned me an excellent supper. Now I owed a decent lunch to my excesses of the night! Gregorio ate standing up on the balcony, wiping out the frying pan with lots of bread, all the time watching me, still shyly, but already smiling. He was handsome, open and simple. He brought us coffee. My host put an arm round his waist. The adolescent let him do so with good grace. He drank the glass of *raki* his master handed him, and remained close beside us, not in the least embarrassed by the hand that lingered on his hip. I had been invited … so we could talk about him. The poor orphan had never known his mother, and was the son of the widowed innkeeper. My old monk was proud of this fine boy. From one *raki* to the next he began to confide in me. He remembered very well having been married. Betrayed by his wife, he became a monk, and on Athos he found the most adorable of wives ... Gregorio said nothing to contradict him; blessed with a friendly nature, this strapping mule-driver's boy never said no. My host, who had been married for a long time, still had fond memories. He got up heavily, opened the chest, and took out a white muslin dress which had belonged to his wife. It was exactly Gregorio's size. By now well and truly drunk, he took the dress carefully in his big hands and held it up against the adolescent. The dress did indeed suit him. A charming Greek peasant woman's dress. Serbian, Serbian! The old man was Serbian, and his runaway wife, a native of Novi Sad, had left him for a miller from Mare. He asked Gregorio to put on the dress. Gregorio, who drew water for him and never said no, took off his clothes. Naked, he put on the unfaithful wife's dress and stood in the middle of the room. Staggering, the old man drew a curtain and plunged us into total darkness. He pushed me against Gregorio, sat down in an armchair, snored loudly and fell fast asleep. I took the adolescent in my arms. We stood in darkness in the middle of the room. The heat was stifling; it must have been noon; the cicadas were singing stridently in the woods. He gently leant his head in the hollow of my shoulder. My fingers made out fine, hard, round hips beneath the slightly rough muslin fabric. He gave me his lips. I drew Gregorio towards the mat and he did not say no.

Had I fallen asleep after lively pleasures? When I came to, Gregorio had disappeared. As for my host, waking badly from his siesta in a foul temper, furious at having thrown Gregorio into my arms, an 'indulgence' he now regarded as a deplorable weakness caused by drunkenness, he had only one wish: for me to leave as quickly as possible. I took the map of Athos out of my pocket and told him I wanted to reach the immaculate peak. The summit of Athos … he thought about it occasionally. But he had long since given up the idea of joining the hermits on the Holy Mountain. He knew he would never leave Chilandari, where he had his habits, his apartment, his memories … Gregorio. I had no memory, I was young and free. Perhaps I would reach the bright marble peak! He wished me success while pushing me politely towards the door.

The mule-drivers were sitting in the entrance to the monastery, in the shade of an archway, looking at the blue sky.

They pointed out the way to Zografos. I took a path lined by walls beyond which rose tall yew trees. The path became steps, then a track along the side of a steep slope, and went over rocks worn down by mules' hoofs. There I made a first stop: already high up, I saw the sea and the Bay of Bulls. Chilandari was now no more than roofs, lost among the yews. I picked up my bag and threw it onto my shoulder. To reach the west coast I had to cross some rugged hills, a foretaste of the mountain. It was early afternoon, the heat was intense, and too much *raki* had taken the strength out of my legs. I was trickling with sweat, I was now no more than a beast struggling under a heavy load. The lace of one of my sandals broke. I sat down to repair it. Two metres away, coiled up in a bush, a large black snake was lying in wait for me. My blood had been boiling, but it turned to ice. I quickly slid over the stones to get away from the reptile, leaving my bag a few paces from its fangs.

It came out of the bush, uncoiled itself, went down to my bag and stopped, resting against it. For a long time we watched each other. With my knees and elbows rubbed raw, stretched out on the hot sharp stones, I was too frightened to feel any pain. Slowly I slid a few metres further down to protect myself from sudden attack. Once I was safer I calmed down. To continue on my route I had to drive the snake away and retrieve my bag. I threw pebbles at it. The big black snake reared up, hissing. A stone hit it right on the head. Getting to my feet I picked up a lump of shale, threw it and missed. But the impact of the large stone against the rock, and the sound of it rolling down through the undergrowth frightened the snake, and it disappeared into the grass.

Danger averted, my first concern was to find a stick. Armed with a makeshift staff I carried on climbing the track, beating the thickets. Each time I stopped, ever higher among the broom and the thorn bushes, I was able to make out an even vaster horizon of ocean, grey with mist under a cloudless sky. For thirty-odd kilometres the shape of the coastline stood out against the calm blue water. The might of the Greek summer accentuated the cicadas' cries. As I approached the top of the hill, legs worn out with fatigue, the insects' song was deafening. The heat from the stony ground was unbearable; but then I went into a wood.

Here the path forked. I looked at the map, which was little more than approximate and symbolic when it came to the precise direction of the paths. Which route through the undergrowth led to Zografos? I chose one as better, and soon left the shade of the trees to head into the thickest part of the long dry grass and chestnut saplings. In a clearing, about twenty bulls, whose black backs and horns were all I could see, were seeking the scanty shade of a few spiky trees. They seemed very placid. Nonetheless, I walked faster.

My track became a wide channel, a sort of trench hollowed deeply out of the dry, red earth. Now covered with thick foliage, it led down like a tunnel of greenery towards wild little valleys. I was expecting to see the first roofs of Zografos at any moment, when I heard the heavy galloping of a bull right behind me. The embankment was too high to get out of the way of a charge. I hurried, and so did the animal. The hard hoofs struck the ground rhythmically, stones crumbled under the beast's weight. It was getting closer. Suddenly I saw it bearing down on me, horns lowered. The greenery formed an arch above my head; dropping my bag, I leapt for a branch, climbed onto it, and settled myself in a tree that jutted out like a bridge over the gulley. The rutting beast passed beneath me, brushing me with its horns! Making an immediate u-turn it returned to the attack, roaring, eyes mad, its muzzle covered with foam. It was a four-year-old, heavy and powerful, black, nose hooked, horns bright. Seeing my bag, it trampled and gored it, snorting loudly. I was out of range of its blows, but none too sure about the strength of the tree to which I owed my safety. It was an old beech, uprooted by the wind, lying against younger trees that had stopped it from falling. Cracking noises worried me; it might collapse, hurling me onto the beast in heat which, for the moment, was ploughing the gulley with its hoofs, raising a cloud of red dust. I did not move from my branch. The dry earth reverberated under the weight of the bull, which came back to my bag and struck it with a mournful bellowing. The impact of the hoofs, the animal's violent movements, its heaving breath, my bag filled with saucepans and metal tins, dragged, mistreated, trampled and thrown against the embankments, created a savage uproar muffled by the dense vegetation. Then suddenly the animal calmed down. It stood still as if stupid, tongue dangling down by my bag, its flanks covered in sweat, red with dust. All of a sudden it urinated; a great stream flowed onto the ground. Then, having quite forgotten me, the bull went away, climbed peacefully back up the ravine and returned to its own kind.

When it was a long way off I got down from my branch, thanking the old tree for its kindness. I owed it my life. Had it waited for years to save me from a bull's charge, and then to die an eternal death in the jungle? No sooner had I set foot on the ground than it collapsed with a crash, blocking the gulley with its venerable trunk and a pile of dead branches. I picked up my bag, damaged by the bull, whose strong smell lingered. Trails of saliva spattered the embankments dented with deep hoof-prints, the air smelt of wild animal, dust and urine. I was going to leave; I went up to the tree, I pressed my lips against its old grey bark. I gave it a kiss of love, gratitude and eternal peace before abandoning it to the mystery of the forests of Athos.

The gulley carried on down towards gorges where the vegetation got thicker all the time. Neither the sea nor Zografos was in sight. I went deeper and deeper into dense jungle overlooked by the high ground covered with woods at the foot of the summit. Other gullies met mine, forming a maze of corridors. The map was no use at all. The certainty that I was well and truly lost became very worrying. I had picked up an ancient pathway paved with old flagstones which were prised apart by strong roots. As I went into a cedar forest it turned into a mere track, passing between rocks, some of which would have definitely fallen into the lower valleys if it were not for the trees they were resting against. Cedars, uprooted by the wind, kept blocking my path along the side of a steep slope, with clay-soil soaked by an unseen spring; it was slippery, dangerous ground. I lost my footing; my bag broke my fall, then slowed a frightening slide towards a sheer drop. One knee dislocated, doubled up with pain, still holding my bag by its cloth handle, I almost passed out … Athos was only present in the oppressive, stormy heat, in the monumental size of hundred-year-old cedars, in heavy silence made more solemn by the singing of the cicadas, and in the occasional lone cry of a bird of prey swooping down from high branches.

The pain eased. I managed to get back on my feet and find my path again. A few metres further down it ran along a rocky little cliff where there was a cave used by the bulls.

In this abandoned part of Athos it was a deep lair, created for their use. At the entrance to this cave, an openwork door, made of gigantic stakes roughly fastened together, had been smashed and partly knocked over onto the earth floor, mingled with dung, trampled and fouled by the beasts, until it was no more than hard black peat marked with hundreds of prints. You could still see large stakes forming an enormous enclosure; shining stakes, polished like ivory where bulls had rubbed their flanks since Byzantium.

I entered this lair with fear and respect. A powerful smell overwhelmed me. No fresh dung, since the bulls only came here in winter. I noticed mangers fixed into the rock, a hayloft cut into the stone. Untold battles seemed to have set the bulls against each other; bedding, which was no more than a rotting dung-heap, had been shaken about; mangers had been pulled apart, torn down, trampled, crushed under furious hoofs. Trails of saliva and patches of blood spattered the rock, in several places cut open by horns. A primitive charm filled this cave; a silence and a cold, holy darkness helped relieve my fatigue: it was almost a temple of Mithras, I thought, gently pressing my lips to a bloodstain. The distant cries of the cicadas reached me faintly; the persistent smell of the bulls went to my head, intoxicating me; the entrance to the cave stood out clearly against the greenery of the jungle.

I went back outside; back to the warm heavy air and the forest smells. The sky was grey, a storm was rumbling dully; the day was getting on. I had to make it to Zografos before night, get out of the woods, make a final effort to find a path, especially since my injured knee hurt atrociously and added to my growing terror, caused by a total loss of feeling. The track must lead somewhere. It ran in among young bamboos; it was just a passage through thick vegetation; here and there were clearings. The grass, brutally flattened by tussling bulls, looked as if it had been scythed. I could not see further than ten metres in this narrow valley used only by beasts. The fact that there was bamboo suggested there was a river nearby; a snake slithered in the grass. Once more gripped by my fear of snakes, I went on slowly. The stormy heat of the day must have been making grass snakes and vipers particularly aggressive. No longer knowing where I was, shaking with fright at the slightest rustle of leaves, terrified by crawling things and hissing noises, I was about to go back to the cave, when in front of me I saw the dry bed of a stream, bare and white. It was like a respite. Its smooth round pebbles could not hide anything.

My footsteps crunched on the shingle and dry stones, which I decided to follow in the hope that they would help me get out of the jungle. The storm was approaching, darkening the sky. Trees washed away by flooding had come to rest against rocky sand-bars, covered with a greyish-pink mud, now cracked by the heat. Further downstream it became a sort of stairway of stone, jammed with dead branches.

At the bottom of the valley, a ford, as it was the middle of June, was no more than a dry bed of sand. To my left, a good wide path through a pine wood must lead to Zografos. I hurried along it; a peculiar green light had taken the place of the bright sunshine, the storm was coming; heavy drops were hitting the treetops. It was a mysterious dark path, with soft, sandy soil, where my footsteps made no sound. At the heart of this wood of very old pines, which gave off an exquisite scent of resin, a lamp was burning at a wayside altar, painted blue and containing an old icon. The rain was already whipping the trees; the wind swept away the dead leaves; a bolt of lightning tore the sky, the light blinded me, followed immediately by a violent thunderclap that shook the whole valley. I hurried on through torrential rain.

Emerging from the wood, I spotted Zografos, a large, fairly recent monastery, an enormous barracks surrounded by cypress trees which were being shaken by gusts of wind. I ran along a little path. I entered the courtyard at the same time as a second thunderclap resounded off the roof. The gutters, overflowing with water, poured torrents onto the flagstones.

A door opened and I was asked to come up to the parlour. Soaked to the skin, my clothes in tatters, I stretched out on a couch. The storm was raging with dull roars and thunderclaps, repeated by the surrounding echoes. They brought me coffee and *raki*. Through a small window I saw the black sky and the bright green forests in the rain. Each explosion of thunder lit up the drawing room, the sound of the water on the roofs was deafening; hailstones rattled against the panes of the little window, whose weak catch threatened to break. Had I caught a cold? I was shivering with exhaustion and fever. I was taken to my room, where I put myself to bed without any supper, while the storm slowly moved away. An old monk sat by my bed and deftly felt my painful knee. He had brought a rusty metal box which he opened with some difficulty. From it he took a honey-coloured ointment, which had the miraculous effect of instantly easing my pain. In the silence that had returned, and the delightful calm that followed the storm, he stayed with me, holding my hand, talking to me in a low voice. Who was I? I did not know. My torn clothes were pitiful to see. Was I poor? I did not know if I was poor. He congratulated me on my detachment and my lack of vanity as regards clothing. He returned to the bad state of my clothes: my shirt was no more than a rag, my espadrilles no longer stayed on my feet … Poor child, poor child, he said. He stood up, opened the door of a tiny room, and dragged out a heavy, carefully padlocked trunk onto the wooden floor.

Poor child, he continued to mutter as he chose a little key from a bunch he had just taken from his pocket. He opened the trunk, and I saw him take out military effects, which he threw one by one onto a table. The trunk also contained an excellent pair of boots, cards, notebooks and binoculars, which he put to one side. The clothes seemed to be my size. He checked by laying them on me, as one takes the measurements of a dead person, for I stayed stretched out on the bed, still trembling with fever. There was a pair of khaki shorts and three shirts of the same colour, with no insignia other than an eagle with outspread wings above a sort of cross in the shape of a swastika. The clothes were almost brand-new, slightly faded by the sun. I thanked him for his kindness and asked him about the origin of these military clothes, which had clearly not been worn for a long time.

Kneeling on the floor by the open trunk that he was still exploring, he answered me in a voice that was slow and solemn, hoarse, a little sad, saying that he rejoiced at this opportunity to show charity by giving me the means to clothe myself decently. My lack of memory explained my question. I would have to have forgotten an awful lot about the century not to know that a war had divided human beings. It had been about twenty years ago, foreign soldiers had come to Athos, busying themselves only with archaeology. There were just a few of them, very correct, very handsome, they had stayed only a year, leaving good memories. One of them, exactly my age, had lodged at Zografos. He had known him well … The dear child had left one day, entrusting him with his trunk, promising to come back and fetch it. They had never seen him again. My good monk gave a deep sigh. His far-off gaze seemed to be back in 1942–43 again, years that reminded me of nothing, but for which he was still nostalgic.

The past meant little to me. I was delighted to see the excellent, almost brand-new clothes I was being offered at just the right moment, and still more amused, I who had no sense of identity, at the idea of putting on the clothes of a boy my age who had disappeared for ever and, in a sense, being that boy for a time! The boots seemed to be my size, and I was given them gladly. I also wanted his identity card, his notebooks, his papers, his binoculars—all the contents of the trunk! He hesitated, showed me his military papers: I might as well—one more incarnation did not matter. So, twenty years later, I wanted to be Eric Strauss, aged twenty-four, native of Munich, Bavaria, student of philosophy, corporal in the Hermann Göring Airborne Division stationed in Heraklion, Crete, assigned to a special mission on Mount Athos ... Such a lack of reserve displeased the old man. I saw in his eyes that he took me for one of those people to whom one gives a little out of charity, and who then shamelessly want everything. Taken by surprise for a moment, his natural goodness put this lack of delicacy down to my extreme poverty. We compromised: he would keep the binoculars in memory of that so very polite, so very courteous young German who seemed to have left many regrets on Athos, and I would take the rest.

He stood up and pushed the trunk back into the depths of the little room. The binoculars in his hand, he came up to me in a fatherly way, took my pulse, shook his head, and then left, assuring me that he would soon bring my dinner. He came back with a tray on which he had arranged a few flowers around a plate of soup. I sat on the bed; he put the tray on my knees, remained standing, watching me eat my supper. Then he wished me goodnight. He headed for the door; suddenly, retracing his steps, half-opening his robe, he took the pair of binoculars I wanted and which he was hiding against his heart. With a kindly smile he dropped them on my sheets and went away, leaving me to my joy at being someone else.

The storm had washed the sky, which was clear and light the following day. I studied my map: Konstamonitou was not far, nor was the west coast. I could get there before noon. I examined my bag, damaged by the bull: tins of instant coffee and bags of sugar had not stood up to the fierce blows from its horns. Only one tin and a little sugar were still usable. I took out what was only good for throwing away, which made room to cram in the clothes, the notebooks and the boots I had been given. I decided to leave Zografos dressed as I had been the day before. Why tear a good military uniform on the brambles of Athos's bad roads? I would change in the woods and arrive properly dressed at the next monastery. Emptied of a dozen tins of coffee, my bag managed to take all Strauss's things. But what a weight to carry up hill and down dale! To get to the top of the Holy Mountain quickly, it would have been better to be free and light, without luggage. I did not have a past: so why burden myself with someone else's memories? I almost left everything behind. But Strauss seemed to be not entirely another person …

And anyway, his maps proved to be more accurate than mine. He had carried out a topographical survey of the region, correcting many errors on the old maps. I no longer hesitated about which path to take, especially since I was leaving the forests for delightful valleys where there was less risk of getting lost.

In front of me lay beautiful meadows. The fresh bright air was a sign that the sea was just beyond the hills. A hot sun was scorching the undergrowth. I stopped by some clear water which ran between flat stones. I took off my clothes; naked beside the stream, I made some coffee, alone, happy in a green jungle. A vast sky shone like a perfect blue dome above my head. Dragonflies, their wings quivering, ready to fly off again—a species I didn't recognise—settled on my hands, on the stones: heavy dragonflies, violet, like flowers. I put water in a little saucepan, poured in some instant coffee and sugar and stirred it with a dried twig. Naked, it was as if I were outside of myself. I was sharing unreservedly in the joy of living.

In this lonely valley, as if by some divine spell, nature exceeded itself. The birds, of every colour, were bigger and more beautiful than elsewhere. Was I in the Paradise of the dragonflies, in countless numbers around the stream, and of the birds of God?

My bag thrown into the grass, the clothes I had taken off, and a saucepan on top of a stone made a humble camp, a symbol of my taste for wandering and my poverty. But was I still poor? I rummaged in the bag and laid out my treasures, Strauss's military effects, maps and notebooks, his boots and his binoculars, excellent black boots which I put on without further ado. I took a few steps, and went into the long grass, still damp with morning dew. Jays were chattering in a thicket; a pair of young buzzards soared in the calm air. They flew away from each other, their flights crossed, they fled each other with a flapping of wings, as if playing a game—then slowly came close again, out of love.

With short boots on I was less afraid of snakes. Naked, I went as far as the edge of the wood, watching the buzzards, which soon swooped down onto a tree with a great sound of feathers whipping the branches. I walked up to the tree, a lone oak in the jungle. They did not fly off: they were not afraid of me. I went back to my little campsite. The young buzzards, the only couple in this peaceful valley, would have made me regret being alone, even with the feminine part of my nature to take my mind off of this solitude in the garden of Eden. But the clothes of a young soldier who had disappeared twenty years before, had given me, in the absence of a wife, the chance, while I wore them, of a metamorphosis. Soon I was dressed as him. The badge, sewn on to one of the pockets of his shirt, was a fine one: an eagle above a fiery wheel.

Lying in the grass, I went through his papers, his notebooks filled with photos and letters.

I had two sisters. A photo, dated 1934, taken by our parents, showed the three of us in a garden in Bavaria. My pretty sisters had long plaits and were standing in front of the Alps and smiling. 1935, a photo of me in the Hitler Youth. I am fifteen; my face glows with a rapturous joy, the wind has dishevelled my long hair. 1936, still in the Hitler Youth; someone has photographed me beside a glider; on the side of a slope, my comrades can be seen holding a cable attached to the front of the plane.

'*Eric, the day he got his glider pilot's licence*'; I recognised Mother's writing. 1938, my sisters, prettier than ever! 1939, at the flying school in Stuttgart. This time I am in the uniform of the Luftwaffe. Photos of the French countryside and of Crete; letters from my mother, notebooks describing my journey, which I decided to reread later.

It must have been ten o'clock in the morning. I gathered up my possessions and headed for Konstamonitou, sad to leave this peaceful valley, telling myself as I went that the myth of the garden of Eden is fundamental to German thought. The Semitic notion of sin is foreign to us; we fight to rediscover Man before the Fall, and to give him victory over the will of all the worn-out races! I suddenly remembered it was 1954. For a few moments I had thought it was 1942! Since my arrival on Athos I had often noticed a sudden burst of time, an undercurrent from the past, sometimes difficult to make out, but undeniable, from details, from little things … and getting more frequent every day; breaks in time, inversions of time, probably connected to the loss of a personal identity. I was dead! Was I dreaming? My adventures on the Holy Mountain were merely the result of my tendencies and my previous lives. So who was dead? Had I been Strauss? Or was Strauss just one possibility for me, among all my likely ones? I must get used to being just a soul, rich with the many lives I had lived—or not lived. For in the world beyond, the possible is as true as all the rest! One certainty made itself clear: I had only crossed a first threshold. My past lives were still exerting all their influence on my behaviour. True death, the ultimate threshold, would come later. If I had had to give a name to these beautiful valleys, to the immaculate peak where I was headed, I would have called them the *Devakhan*: the land of happy souls. The word *Devakhan* came from the vocabulary of Hinduism. So who had studied Hinduism? Strauss, at Munich University? Strauss, the philosophy graduate? Or someone else I was, someone whose name I did not know, and who was walking along a path through a wood in the cool shadows?

I spotted Konstamonitou: a small, very rustic-looking monastery. It was like a long, ancient farmhouse with a grey stone roof and half-ruined balconies, just visible above the long green grass. The air smelt of new-mown hay. Tame bulls were grazing in a meadow enclosed by fences made of young, roughly-cut pine. I pushed open a gate. Under a vast blue sky I crossed the meadow, keeping my distance from the bulls. Another gate led to a decent cobbled pathway. I seemed to recognise these enormous pastures and this path which led to some cedars. Had I been to Konstamonitou during the war, in 1942? Or was coming to this monastery just a dream, born of the undercurrent of another past, in the same way that I imagined myself as Strauss? I must give up any idea of identity, see time break loose without being surprised by it! I was getting used to this new state, even enjoying it, as one breathes clearer air at high altitude. Dead, I felt lightened, freer and happier than on earth. The sky was blue, I was young. With no regrets, I made do without time, I made do without myself.

I was not so sure about the welcome that might await me in this old monastery. The Germans had left good memories; but this eagle, this swastika sewn over my heart, could mean there were surprises in store.

At the far end of the path, the cedars shaded pigsties where black piglets wallowed in the mire. As I got closer they gave shrill cries, as if they hated Germans. The rusticity and great age of Konstamonitou became more apparent all the time. The entrance, dark and dirty, was like the entrance to a barn; the door had recently been painted bright blue, a celestial colour that contrasted unexpectedly with the sorry state of the roofs and the walls. On this June morning under the cedars, a monk was splitting wood. He put down his axe and watched me approach, wide-eyed. When the piglets had stopped their noise I greeted him politely. He answered with indistinct grunts. He seemed a bit simple. I showed him the parchment giving me the right to enter all the monasteries on Athos.

He looked very Christian, very bemused, grimy and utterly stupid.

"German, German?" he stammered.

"Yes, German," I answered curtly. He was getting on my nerves.

He was not unfriendly. He was just a moron. I told him I wanted to visit Konstamonitou.

"Visit?"

"Yes, visit, look at."

"Ah, visit … "

I could have hit him. He stuck his axe in the block and asked me to follow him. Still in the shade of the cedars, which formed a sort of wood in the middle of the fields, he led me towards a pen surrounded by heavy boards. For a moment I thought the poor man wanted to show me his pigs first. A violent jolt shook the planks, followed by galloping noises in the mud. I went closer. A large wild boar was studying me, an enormous beast with sparse bristles and bright eyes. It butted the enclosure a second time. A sharp, pungent smell rose from its sty.

"Wild boar, wild boar!"

"I can see it's a wild boar," I told the monk.

We went into the monastery. The poor man lived there alone, and he had let it go until now it was no more than a farm. The courtyard was a sea of mud where manure rotted. Flies were buzzing, wasps were swarming round some old vines; a calf came into the courtyard, perfectly at home, and followed us to a little red-brick church, where he opened the door for me; it was painted blue as well.

He stood back to let me go in. My boots echoed on the loose floor tiles as I walked towards the icons of a humble Deësis, painted by a clumsy hand. The church was cold, with low arches, decorated with naive frescoes which seemed to have been blackened by fire long ago. Everything was small at Konstamonitou, simple and poor. The iconostasis was just an old, primitive construction of gilded wood, eaten by worms. A Byzantine Christ, wild and sad, kept watching me. The Virgin had the look of a silly peasant woman, and John the Baptist that of a lunatic dressed in clothes made of camel-hair, taking his madness round with him among the rocks of a naively-portrayed desert. Christianity: a religion for little people! I rejected it with all my youthful strength. The grandeur of Byzantine art touched me, the Gospel annoyed me; gold attracted me, Judeo-Levantine pessimism horrified me. Christianity, the religion of the simple-minded, traitors to Europe, was to be destroyed for the good of Aryan thought! "Fine," I said to the monk, taking a last glance at the humble Deësis, and left, my boots still making a loud noise.

"Come with me," he said.

Lifting the skirt of his dirty black robes he set off up a steep wooden staircase, with very high steps, almost a ladder, which led to the one upper storey of this poor monastery. We went down a corridor. I thought he was going to offer me coffee in his kitchen, when he opened a door on to a balcony, whose many little windows looked on to the forest. There were small cupboards, with lots of drawers filled with powder paint. The rough floor was spattered with blue, ochre and pink. This was the long-abandoned holy studio of an icon painter. The monk made a gesture of wonderment. "*Archeo Katigitis tis Zographikis*!" he cried. A very old painter, a master … had worked here! You could not wish to see a lovelier studio, with its delightful little windows, the small panes giving a gentle light. Curtains of fine material, faded by the sun, ran along little cords. Everything was fragile and delicate in this cramped studio, hovering above the kitchen garden. Fine-pointed brushes lay at the bottom of the drawers and on the window sills. Several copper pots were still filled with powdered gold. I lingered. I was moved. An old man had worked here for a very long time. You could imagine his patience and meticulousness, his taste for order, his slow, measured movements. The smell of glue hung in the air, impregnating the carved wood; but more than that there was a nameless charm, which might have been the love of good painting; perhaps you would call it the beneficial conditions of silence, humility, light, patience and solitude which are necessary for painting a masterpiece. This affected me personally. A part of my being loved Byzantine painting, although I could not see what the connection was that linked this attraction for gold and icons to Aryan thought. In the past, had I been a Christian, had I painted icons? Had I been this master or his disciple? The memory of it had been wiped away during the centuries. All I had left was a deep desire to touch this gold powder, these divine blues and ochres. Quietly I left the studio, with its views of the white marble slopes of the Holy Mountain beyond the pastures and the green forests. Back in the courtyard, rather ashamed of my harshness to the poor monk, I kissed his hand with a filial, probably Slavic gesture. Then I hurried away, leaving him to his logs and his black piglets.

A rugged path led down to the sea. I walked with light steps, happy with this perpetual wandering which, towards midday, brought me to a shoreline.

How many days was it since I arrived on Athos? Four or five? I would have thought more. Once again, the feeling of a vast expanse of time, constantly interrupted, uncertain, delicious—almost an absence of time! At the very least, with every step I took, I felt time was being modified because of the proximity of the Divine. At that moment there was not a boat in sight. The horizon was very blue. A fisherman's house. No one around. A jetty jutted out into the water, so clear that I could see the shingle beneath the surface a long way out, right up to the first plunging drops, where they disappeared into green depths. I took off my clothes and my boots. The stones burnt in the hot noonday sun, the light blinded me. I bathed; but, racked with hunger and quite weak, I dare not lose my footing. Returning to the shore with its large pebbles, very white, like bones piled up beside the motionless sea, I put on my Luftwaffe clothes again, and looked in vain for a spring. The house, its door double-locked, was reached by a small set of steps and had a veranda on the front, covered by a plank roof which shaded me from the beating sun. I lay down on the rough floorboards. There was a table, chairs, bundles of garlic hanging from the beams. Would the fishermen come back tonight? Or ever? I was alone on the west coast. And without water! I fell asleep. What did I have to fear on Athos? The calm sea lapped softly over the shingle of the deserted beach; not a cloud in the blue Greek sky; not a sound, except for the gentle surf.

A sudden, loud crash woke me from my nap. Mule-drivers, back from the hills, dumped a load of logs onto the stones of the beach. They found me lying in front of their door.

"You German?"

Still half-asleep from my siesta, not quite knowing what I was doing on the floor—and even less who I was—I accepted without protest the first role I was given to play:

"Yes, German."

I stood up so they could get past. They went into their poor house and suggested I share their modest supper. We had dinner on the balcony, in view of the sea. I told them I wanted to reach the summit of Athos. As I might have expected, they tried to dissuade me. I insisted. They told me I had come much too far north, that I must go back to Kariés. The sun was disappearing below the horizon of the sea; they smoked fine Greek cigarettes, played cards. At nightfall they brought a bed out onto the balcony for me, and went off to sleep on the sand.

Delighted to be alone at last, stretched out on this uncomfortable bed, one shoulder on my bag, I looked at the sea, very black in the moonless night: the Aegean Sea, flecked with white foam. A great warmth rose up from the shore. I got some cool air from the waves each time they touched the stones … A mighty silence followed every soft murmur of the gently-sifted pebbles … The water swept in again, untiring in its divine determination to wash this beach for eternity.

The sturdy struts and beams of my wooden balcony stood out dimly against the sky. The night was beautiful, harmonious, full of stars! The song of the tide died way, only to begin again with a delicacy beyond measure. The admirable monument of the stars and constellations shone above the heavy marble of the smooth warm water. On this summer night, on this balcony, a few steps from the sea, I was happy in a land I loved, my soul's true homeland, a place where dreams were stored. I did not want to sleep, so much did this delicious night keep my eyes open in the depths of a darkness that was only interrupted by the gentle motion of the surf.

I still did not know who I was. Should I hope to re-emerge from this state of gentle alienation? I was dead, and quietly welcomed, fed, housed, passed from hand to hand like a soul forever rescued and protected; a soul that will not return to the world of men, and which must slowly get accustomed to a new life that still surprises and pleases it … A stronger wave swept onto the shore, thundering on the shingle, hurling a tide of foam against the beach. The wind got up; a coolness breathed out by the sea stroked my face. I closed my eyes on the rickety bed and fell asleep, while the mules, left to wander, tinkled their little bells far away in the countryside.

By the time the sun was just getting up, I had left the mule-drivers.

I walked along the seashore. A large staff that I found on the sand helped me over the stones, which kept shifting under my feet. The west coast proved to be steep and dry, and often fell sheer to very deep water. So I had to risk going on the wet, slippery rocks, pounded by the waves, where my stick was useful again; or else climb up into the hills, which were full of the calls of the cicadas, before getting back onto a beach after struggling for an hour. At the end of the day I had made little progress. Not a boat out at sea; a wild, uninhabited coast, difficult to negotiate. It was nearly evening. Alone with the sea and half-lost, I was ready to sleep on the sand when I saw the opening to a cave at the far end of a wide bay.

A camp seemed to have been set up in this chilly cavern. Heavy stones, which had fallen from the roof, had been used to make a hearth. Blackened by the fire, they were still hot. Next to them were a bundle of cheap-looking clothes and a tin of salt standing on the pebbles. The sole inhabitant of this sad cave could not be very far away. Re-emerging from the gloomy hideout, I walked barefoot onto the shore, carrying my boots.

A boat had just landed. A very thin man, ageless, was at the oars. He asked me who I was. I replied that I did not know, that I was dead, without water and exhausted. He passed me a two-handled jug made of rose-pink clay. When I had quenched my thirst he put it back under a seat and asked me to get into the boat. We put out to sea. Some distance from the beach, where the sea was very calm at the close of day, he gestured to me that I had to take the oars and row slowly towards a marker floating on the water. He grabbed it and gradually reeled in a long line, which he coiled round a piece of wood. Not a single fish had taken on the old hooks, which he stuck one by one into a cork. Another line, brought up further out to sea, proved as devoid of any catch as the first. The hooks were completely bare. The poor man lived by his fishing! He looked extremely weak, gentle and sad, in despair because of his loneliness and poverty. He took a bucket with a glass bottom in it and, leaning out over the water, studied the sea bed which was plainly visible through the clear water: a maze of rocks, hollowed-out into dark corridors. Lying within reach across the boat was a long pole with a barbed trident on the end. Several times I thought he was going to use it. Yes, he was moving his hand to pick it up … Since I was hungry as well, I followed his slightest move with interest. When the boat got too far away from the maze he winked at me to get me to change my stroke with the old oars that I was dipping lightly into the warm, smooth water, peaceful and violet at this late hour. Tired of a fruitless search, he threw the bucket angrily into the boat and, sitting down in the stern with his head in his hands, seemed lost in thought.

Suddenly making up his mind, he opened the door of a small chest, a little store-cupboard full of ropes. He took out a knotted handkerchief and untied it to reveal a strange blue stone which he seemed to regard as the greatest of treasures; a rather crumbly stone, very bright blue. He gazed at it with admiration and with sadness. After much hesitation he broke off a tiny piece, which he put on the seat in front of him. The poor man put the stone back in the handkerchief and hid it in the cupboard. Meanwhile we had been drifting. Rowing noiselessly, we returned to our position above the shallows. Again he plunged the windowed bucket into the water to get a better view of the green rocks, the motionless seaweed three metres below the heavy boat, swaying on a slight swell.

He gripped the fragment of blue stone in his fingers and dropped it into the water when the place seemed to suit him. I leant over the side … It drifted down slowly into the clear water, dissolving very quickly and leaving a long blue trail. It hit the bottom and immediately formed a small cloud, still of an intense blue.

Fish appeared from all sides. They came out of the underwater caves and gathered round the cloud. Octopus, irresistibly attracted, emerged from their lairs and crawled over the rocks. The poor fisherman picked up the trident. With his first thrust he ran through an octopus, which he brought to the surface. He pulled it from the trident and threw it in the bottom of the boat. With another lunge he brought up another octopus, together with a good-sized fish caught in the weapon's prongs. A third octopus joined the first two; they wriggled like snakes in the dirty water that lapped at the bottom of the boat, where the fish was thrashing about violently. Then nothing. Once the cloud had dissolved, few fish or octopus stayed in reach of the trident. We remained on watch. The water was getting dark, night was coming on quickly now. The beach, which was a fair way off, was no more than a faint line of pink sand, arcing round at the foot of enormous hills that were full of the cries of insects.

He gestured at me to head back to shore. The crickets' song got closer, deafening in the warm, calm night. There must have been thousands of them in the bushes and the branches of the wild olive trees, scratching away beneath the stars. The boat bumped onto the sand and we got out, wading in the lukewarm surf. With only the night sky for light, laden with still-live octopus which were winding their tentacles round our wrists, with our jar of water and fish carried by the gills, we arrived at the cave. I heard him snap a few small branches, I saw the quick flash of a lighter. With a lively crackling sound, pretty flames lit up the cave. There were some dead trees there, strangely whitened by being in the sea for a long time. He threw one onto the stones that served as his hearth. For a few minutes the fire seemed to be almost smothered by the weight of wood. The cave got dark again; then, a huge flame drove away the shadows. The scrawny silhouette of the fisherman stood out against the brightness of the fire. Still with the infinite sadness that characterised his every gesture, he prepared the octopus, striking them against the stones, the supple, gleaming tentacles slapping like bunches of leather thongs. Having emptied them of ink, he carried them to the sea, along with our one fish. I followed him silently on the warm sand, not wanting to be on my own in that unhappy cave, and because the black water attracted me, fascinated me, so powerful and calm under the starry sky.

The silent fisherman walked into the surf, trousers rolled up his thin calves. He gutted the fish, threw the entrails into the water, cleaned off the scales with a knife, then washed the flesh. Back in the cave he laid the octopus and the fish on the burning hot coals, while, kneeling on the shingle, I opened my bag. A gleam of envy flashed in his eyes at the sight of my provisions. It was a starving man, deprived of everything, who watched me fill a little saucepan with fresh water, bring it to the hot coals, and pour in coffee and sugar. Using a stick, he turned over the octopuses, which were hissing on the fire. Soon our supper was ready. He put out the fire, which plunged us back into the semi-darkness of the fine summer night.

We ate our meal outside the cave, stretched out on the warm sand, in sight of the sea that was as black as the ink from our octopus meat. Propped up on my elbows beside him, I held out my saucepan, filled with very strong coffee, which he drank greedily to the last drop. I questioned him. He seemed slightly mad, lost in loneliness. Seized with pity I gave him my cigarettes, more than twenty packets. He thanked me, almost in tears. He talked: he was dead and knew it. A fisherman by trade, he had lived on Athos for a long time, alone in this cave. There were not many fish in the sea, and his equipment was out of date. He suffered constantly from hunger. In the chest on the boat he had found the blue stone that attracted the fish and the octopuses. He only used it in dire circumstances, when fishing was fruitless, when the hunger got too dreadful. Although he only broke off a tiny piece each time, the stone was being used up. He saw the time coming when there would be none left. And the wick of his lighter was getting shorter as well. Soon, no more fire, no more fish! What crime was he atoning for? He would have liked to return to the world of men. He missed his wife and his children; he had a son of my age. Hunger, hunger, he repeated, touching my bare shoulders. He came closer and sank his teeth into the nape of my neck. I could feel the poor fisherman weeping. He was hungry for me. Taking him in my arms on the warm sand, between the murmuring sea and the call of the crickets, that night I was for him both food, and his wife and son.

The stars were going out one by one in a sky that was already green. A pale gold heralded the coming dawn. Everything seemed to be suspended, scarcely born, delightful in the hands of God. A great silence had woken me. The insects had fallen silent. The sea, calm as a lake, was sleeping peacefully. Resting on my elbows on the shore, I looked at the poor fisherman, stretched out on his stomach, head in his arms. Dead, this simple man carried on his humble trade as a fisherman every day as though in a dream, not wanting to venture any further in the Land of Souls. As for me, in the clear dawn a lucky premonition was urging me to leave. Again I heard a call from the forests of the Holy Mountain. Many spells had delayed me. Could I hope for other magic, this time more favourable? In a hurry to go to my master, I left the fisherman to his deep sleep. I walked away across the damp sand, which the sea, waking with the rising sun, was caressing with its first cool waves.

Around ten o'clock in the morning, I saw a blue and white caique at anchor in a little creek. I was taken aboard, the engine was started. We headed along the west coast. Soon we were in sight of Dochiariou, whose roofs and Byzantine domes reflected in the smooth water which our stern was slicing through. We tied up at the end of a jetty, and chests were unloaded, enough time for me to climb up to the monastery, enjoying the sound of my black boots ringing on the flagstones of the courtyards. I was happy to be alive! On this fine June morning my Luftwaffe uniform suited me well. It symbolized my denial of the Levantine Christ … Had I been a Christian? Perhaps elsewhere, and in other times? They were calling me from the caique. It was moving away from the quay. We continued sailing, keeping a short distance from the rocks and the beaches. We passed Xenophontos, Panteleimon. Almost straight away I saw the little port of Dáfni.

"Kariés, Kariés," the sailors shouted, pointing out a path that went up the side of dry stony slopes.

It was a rough path, and I struggled along it under the hot afternoon sun. I was given water at the monastery of Xiropotamou. At nightfall I arrived in Kariés, too late to ask for hospitality at the nearby monastery of Koutloumousiou, whose door would be closed at that time of night.

So I went to find the inn I had already been to. As far as I could remember it was at the top of a steep, narrow alley-way. There was mysterious activity going on in the little streets of Kariés. Lots of monks were coming and going in their black robes. I let myself be carried along by the tide of passers-by. The yellow flames of the paraffin lamps were being lit one by one in the grocery shops of this large village so near to the steep slopes of the Holy Mountain. I caught sight of the bright marble peak, very close, beyond the rooftops, whose heavy carved beams jutted out above the upper storeys and wooden balconies. It was an odd crowd I was mixing with, apparently without them seeing me. These anchorites, these vagrants, these white-bearded *Igumenoi* looked as if they had walked out of the frescoes in their churches, and had to climb back into them later that night. Their very names were those of the saints they worshipped, and whose gestures and bearing they had: Dimitrius, Pachomius, Athanasius. I saw them, these Moses, these Noahs, these Jobs and Melchizedeks, the apostles Peter and Paul, the ones Rublev painted in the icons of Kiev, those whom God alone could imagine, these worshippers of the Lord, their hair and beards all tangled, a goatskin bag over one shoulder!

In the twisting alley-ways, robust hermits from the nearby hills went into grocery shops with a determined step, met friends, cried out with joy, leant their staves against a doorway, and began endless conversations in the soft warm light of the lamps that faintly lit the shelves and counters piled with bags of sugar, tins of food, drums of oil and rolls of material. A smell of spice and pepper floated in the balmy air. A sewing machine whirred away at the back of a barber's shop, where a kind of *salon* was in progress: good monks found the company of others, and were laughing heartily. Climbing three tall steps I entered this peculiar hairdressers where people were drinking coffee, selling hammocks, rakes and forks, and someone was stitching a robe. I went in simply for the pleasure of it, not wanting anything. Everyone went quiet when I appeared. The sewing machine stopped immediately. They gave me friendly smiles. I did not want any hammocks, I didn't want to buy anything. I stood in the doorway for a moment, then went out again and mingled with the crowd. Uncertain of my own existence, had I only wished to be seen? A convoy just down from the forests was making its way with difficulty through the narrow streets. The mules' hard, pointed hoofs rang on the cobbles. The clear sound of their little bells brought with it some of the freshness of the Holy Mountain, whose pure summit dominated the whole of Kariés, this huge trading post with little internal courtyards full of piles of logs, firewood and freshly-cut beams, which gave off an exquisite smell of resin, with, here and there, at the bend in an alley, far away from the light, a hidden supply of shadows, a stable haunted by old spells, or smelling of fresh grass and straw. Kariés, this village without women, its tiny shops filled at nightfall by the bearded monks and the mule-drivers of Athos, had not only been known to me for centuries, but also reminded me of similar villages I had known in Asia, in the foothills of other sacred mountains, in other climates, and which I could not place in any exact cycle of incarnations or dreams.

But in this one I suddenly saw my inn and went in. I sat down on a bench at the far end of the room, at a long table covered with a waxed cloth, and ordered supper. They brought me a bowl of soup and a glass of *raki*, followed by a steaming dish of courgettes, fried fish and olives. The flame of a powerful paraffin lamp hanging from one of the beams, together with the fires of the stoves, made the intense heat of the fine summer evening almost unbearable. Three mule-drivers were drinking resinous wine and talking quietly. A monk came in to smell the good smells of the meat simmering in the frying pans. He dipped a finger in the sauces, which he tasted with an air of detachment, as if merely in passing. He tore off a small piece of meat, which he swallowed greedily; then wiped his beard with the back of his hand and went off quite calmly without offering to pay a penny, congratulating the landlord on the quality of his sauces. A novice, with beautiful girlish eyes and long hair falling over his shoulders, appeared from the crowd that was passing the door, went into the kitchen and came out with a copper tray full of cups of coffee, which he took to the good monks who, in the hairdressing salon across the street, were still laughing and chatting to the whirr of the sewing machine. As for me, I was drunk on *raki*, heat, and even more intoxicated at the thought of knowing I was close to the immaculate peak of the Holy Mountain, which attracted me like a powerful magnet. Would my master come to me? I hoped so; I was sure of it. Recognising him instantly, I would catch sight of him in the doorway of the inn, silently watching me. Without a word, without a gesture, he would command me to follow him into the Sacred Forest. I kept my eye on the street, the vagabonds and the wise men going by. I was sure I would see him before long. Tired from my long wait, I left the table and washed my hands in a copper basin fixed to a wall; I splashed water on my face, I combed my untidy hair. I looked at myself in a mirror … face burnt by the sun, hair dusty, looking happy, determined, a little feverish. I went back to my place. As the night went on, the bustle in Kariés died down; shops were shut; the sewing machine stopped its tireless tic-tac. My master did not come. The mule-drivers went off to find their beasts. The narrow street was empty; not a single footstep sounded now. I was alone with the landlord, who sat down beside me.

He had recognised me, and treated me well.

"Well then, so you're German now!" he said with a laugh.

I soon told him about my wanderings and how I had inherited a Luftwaffe uniform. Not knowing who I was, being German by chance for a time did not displease me.

"There's no such thing as chance in the next world," he answered me sententiously, pointing a finger at the ceiling! He added that the Germans had not left good memories everywhere. I ran the risk of being taken for an old enemy, attracting some hostility, even being stoned by uncouth mule-drivers. Yes, stoned! "It would be wise," he went on, "to get rid of this Luftwaffe uniform. It might cause you problems." At which he asked if I had any money on me? I searched my pockets: I had twenty five drachmas left.

"That's not much," he said, feeling the military fabric to make sure it was almost brand-new. Did I still have my old clothes? I could see the seasoned trader appearing, and was not really surprised when he offered me a thousand drachmas for my German Air Force uniform. Not wishing to be defrocked, nor to be stoned by stupid mule-drivers who took me for someone else, and as I was not attached to some borrowed identity, I accepted the price without haggling. Then, to seal our agreement, my Greek landlord gave me a last glass of *raki*.

After a moment's silence, I told him that it was a pleasure to be back in his inn again, so close to the dark cedar forests where I wanted to rejoin my master.

"If he even exists!" He did not hide from me that this search could be long! Or very short! Only God knew. The Great Ancients might oppose this plan, so it was best if I didn't talk about it in any of the taverns on Athos. "Don't worry, I can keep a secret," he added in a low voice, after making sure we were alone. To hear him talk I might have been an old dreamer, someone who has divine blood in him, who has strange, noble thoughts that ordinary mortals cannot understand; one of those daring souls who are forever talking about distant lands, about unknown gardens high in the mountains. I was one of those people who are treated as mad, often wrongly, for these gardens and mysterious high slopes may actually exist somewhere; or else, sadly, they exist only in their dream-world and thus have no reality, even in the hereafter. I replied that I was sure I had already lived on Athos, and was relying on a host of previous existences and memories to find the master whose call I could hear, whom I loved and had known for all eternity. He wished me luck, but told me that I would soon be back in Kariés. He gave me a thousand drachmas and advised me to get some sleep.

We went through the courtyard. A wooden staircase, then a balcony, led to one of the upper bedrooms of this old inn. He lit a candle, put it on a little marble mantelpiece, and left me, asking the Virgin and Christ to grant me a peaceful sleep.

I went back to the balcony and stayed there a very long time. Was it being so close to the pure marble peak, the altitude? The intense heat that had lasted until late in the evening gave way to air that was almost cold. I leant on the balustrade and took deep breaths of this fresh clear air that smelt of resin, and rested from my long day's walk. The forests stood out black against a sky white with nebulous cloud and twinkling stars. Everything was still in the perfect tranquillity, in the silence of the night, occasionally broken by hoof-beats from the mules in a nearby stable. A slight gust of wind blew out my candle, whose glow was bothering me. Now I could see the surrounding buildings more clearly. They were very old, with architraves and beams, the gardens enclosed by walls and, on the other side of the courtyard, the stable where the mules were moving about, an old stable with a wooden door painted red, strengthened by iron bars and nails. In the peace of this beautiful summer night, fine smells of incense from mysterious chapels mingled with the strong scent of dung, resin and hay which permeated the whole of Kariés. Beyond the gardens there must have been open meadows, for I could hear the tinkling of a bell, then others, further away, answering it very clearly. I liked Kariés, and I would have decided to stay in this strange village, where so many distant memories came back to me, if my spirit of adventure had not been urging me to climb the high slopes of the Holy Mountain. The call was becoming irresistible. I knew the laws of the next world. In my few days of wandering I had already used up a large part of a powerful karma that had weighed on me since the start of my death. The laws in the Land of the Spirits were odd: not one coincidence, not a single chance meeting! A chain of events brought about by my former lives, an almost mathematical prediction of most of my tendencies. So who had I been to experience so many joys on this side of life? My past existences were still a mystery to me. It seemed I had not been very happy in the world of men, and that my inexpressible happiness in the Land of Souls was compensation for much suffering. Whatever the case, I wanted to go higher up the mountain; as if light-hearted, I could hope to cross the final thresholds! The best and the holiest part of my nature, which had also been formed slowly over many centuries, wanted to be fulfilled in the hereafter as well. Its time had come! My true self was burning with impatience at the thought of rejoining its master, and I would have gone straight away if I had not thought it was a good idea to have a few hours' rest before setting out on the rough paths of the Sacred Forest.

I went back to my room and lit the candle again. Lying across my bed, a young black cat, like the one I had stroked at Chilandari, was purring softly on the sheets. It got up as I approached, seeming to recognise me, and made a great fuss of me while I was taking off my Luftwaffe clothes. Was it the same one, or another? Or a second appearance in the after-life of a cat I had loved in the world of men, probably more than the men, and whose memory kept pursuing me? I was wise enough already, and too happy by nature, to waste time trying to explain the unexpected reappearance of this friendly cat. I ran my fingers along its back, it rubbed itself against me. I got into bed. It snuggled into the hollow of my shoulder, and I closed my eyes but could not sleep, for I was eager to set off for the mountain. The innkeeper's words about the Great Ancients' possible opposition to my plan to climb the upper slopes, which was more or less forbidden, came back to me. Could I trust him to be discreet? He would betray me at dawn, I was suddenly sure of it! As if guessing my secret fears, the cat jumped off the bed, left the room, and miaowed on the wooden balcony. I got dressed as fast as I could, putting on my old clothes, and leaving the military things I had sold the night before on the bed. The boots might be useful on the mule-drivers' tracks.

With great honesty I reckoned they must be worth two hundred and fifty drachmas, which I put on the marble fireplace where it could be seen. I snuffed out the wick of the candle between my fingers. Then quietly, I left the inn.

In the lovely silence at the end of the night, I walked along several alley-ways with the cat going ahead of me. Stealthily it leapt, and ran over the grassy paving stones, crept along the top of walls, and kept turning round and calling me to follow. In this part of Kariés, the heavy scent of wisteria drifted from the sleeping gardens and filled the still air. A cock crowed from a distant farm.

Still guided by the cat, and by the faint light of the stars, I went boldly down the hundred steps of the last street, which led to a bridge. I set off along a track into the enchanted woods.

PART TWO

Monastery of Grégorios

IV

JOSHUA, THE SACRED FOREST, AND THE VOYAGE TO IERISSOS

SINCE NIGHT ENDED I had been climbing higher and higher into the forest. I had left behind the charred ashes of the woodcutters' last camps, the heaps of rotting wood shavings, the huts made from cut branches built between hundred-year-old trees. A fast-flowing river roared between the rocks, which in places were submerged beneath its strong, steady current. I went down to the bank and walked into the icy water. This was now the only possible way through the forest, which was so dense it was becoming impassable.

Daybreak, pink and gold, lit up the white marble of Athos. With every step I took, the nearness of it kindled my inexpressible joy at having entered the forbidden woods. A light summer mist lay in the wild gorge, unknown to mortals, where songbirds watched my struggle to make headway through the clear cold river, which here and there formed calm pools that reflected dense thickets of black pine and ancient cedars. In up to my waist, in danger of being knocked over by the strength of the water, was I really alone in the holy forest? I had a feeling I was accepted, judged by the trees who were wiser and happier than men! An incredible secret invaded my clear consciousness: God was roaming the forest! At sunrise He went from branch to branch; He visited His faithful, the great, peaceful trees who had known Him for all eternity and who worshipped Him in silence.

Walking through the icy water using a long pole to tread along the bottom of this violet gorge still shrouded in mist, I was reborn without fear in the hands of God. The strong current foamed against my thighs and washed me clean of life. So who had I been in my many lives to return so easily to this peace, like the peace at the beginning of the world? For the span of a single bird's call I saw myself back in Byzantium and in unhappy Europe, an alchemist stubbornly listening to the powerful voice of the Lord of Light, knowing His laws and loving Him in secret. I was not a man like other men! Unlike Adam I had not renounced my Creator! Old as the world, I was one of those who, through the ages, never forgot the sweetness and the strength of the primordial state, which is that of the angels.

Certain of my deep love of God, which had lasted for a thousand years, deafened by the constant singing of the waves bouncing over the many rock ledges, I went higher and higher up the mountain. I entered the region where the hermits lived; the forest got colder and more silent. Near the foaming water, I passed notches cut into the living rock. It was a kind of ancient staircase, worn away, hewn as if by giants, green with damp and marked at almost every turn with little blue-painted wayside altars, semi-abandoned in the sacred peace of the woods. The pale moon was in its last quarter, and shone among the branches. The birds had fallen silent. Far from lifting with the coming of day, the banks of white vapour at the bottom of the valley were getting thicker, and now hid the river. Its roaring got fainter as I climbed through the woods. I carried on up the ancient staircase, which did not stray far from the thundering of the water. I paused; standing on an overhang of rock I looked at the plunging landscape, frosty and pure, laid out before me. The marble and the cedars of the Holy Mountain stood out like islands above the mist.

It melted away slowly, revealing the powerful jungle that covered the banks of the river. Silent doves left the mysterious upper foliage, hovered in the blue air, and came back to their beloved forest. They settled on the branches, beating the green leaves with their wings, and went right into the thickest parts of the woodland, knowing all the secret passages that led to caves. Then, lower down, a little hermitage appeared, with its wooden roof and balcony, and its walls of dried earth. Here the river formed several pools whose stillness contrasted with the choppy little waves that leapt over the stones.

He was washing a saucepan in the fast current, sometimes knocking it against a rock. A metallic sound, unusual in the Sacred Forest, mingled with the roar of the river. He was an old man, dressed like a monk, with long hair and a beard. I got close enough to make out his face, that of a plain and simple gardener. I had a horror of simple people: the legacy of my distant past, a thousand years of refusing to believe in the virtue of humble folk. Which is another way of saying I was not a Christian, and knew it. He was just some old fool in this incredible paradise, the gorges of Athos. He carried on scrubbing his saucepan with a handful of gravel, then banged it on the rock before plunging it back into the clear water. When it was clean and shiny he climbed up a path leading to his rustic balcony, where doves were settling. Hidden in the greenery, I watched him from the other side of the river. Barefoot, he came back to the river-bank with a bundle of laundry which he set about washing energetically, sleeves rolled-up, kneeling by the water like a washerwoman. He slapped it on the stones, rinsed it, stood up, trampled on it vigorously, wrung it out, and went back to his house. The good man hung his poor laundry out to dry on string stretched between the beams of the balcony, which was decorated with white carnations growing in rusty old tin cans which he watered with a coffee pot. He disappeared into the house, which had the distinct look of a long hut lost in the woods. He re-emerged around eleven o'clock, sat down on a bench in the shade of an arbour and told his beads as the cicadas sang. A child came down to the stream carrying the fine saucepan, which he filled with ice-cold water. He dawdled on the rocks, threw pebbles into the waves, then climbed merrily up the lovely path where bees were buzzing, the occupants of hives in nearby caves.

Later, after a little nap, the old man hoed his garden under an overhang of the rocky cliffs, barely visible beneath the abundant vegetation. I saw him coming and going among his flowers and vegetables, a small hoe in his hand, wearing a big straw hat and an apron tied tightly round his ungainly hips.

All day long I watched them, without wanting to show myself. They must have had a siesta, as I did not see them during the hottest hours of the day. Their door was shut; the cicadas sang. He was just a peasant; it was obvious from his movements, his bearing. I did not believe that wisdom was to be found in idiocy. To think I had climbed so high up the mountain in search of a master, only to meet just one simple man! The great hermits of the Holy Mountain had gone for ever, with no one to succeed them but good honest gardeners. I had arrived too late in the Sacred Forest. Up until the last century, wise men had lived in these high places; but since then, neglected Athos was reverting to jungle, to simplicity, and was now just frequented by ignorant monks. I was beset by stormy thoughts, anger and disappointment, and, more profoundly, a mad craving to take his place. I liked his hermitage of wooden planks and dry earth, this long balcony beside the water; and the child looked beautiful. What I wanted more than anything was for the old man to disappear: let him go back to his God, the carpenter from Nazareth, and leave this place to me! Yes, I wished him dead. Or at least that he would go away. I wanted to settle here and live as I pleased on these wild, beautiful heights, alone with the child, chopping wood in the forest and building a boat. I ought to have been on my guard for deep echoes from the Land of the Spirits: that which one most desires … unfailingly happens! Did I guess that later on I would live in this region of caves, very poor and alone? Did I suspect it … even for a moment, for the time it took a wave to whisper? But I was young, carefree, happy!

They reappeared late in the afternoon and drank coffee together on a bench. In the cool air, the hermit went back to his garden while the child broke up dry wood. Darkness slowly took over the jungle, which vanished among the evening shadows, leaving just an incredible perfume of flowers and leaves as a reminder of its presence, mingled with a strong smell of sludge from the stagnant backwaters. When it was completely dark, I crossed the river and knocked at the door.

It was the boy who answered. Had he spotted me when he was fetching water? Accustomed to living deep in the woods, had he, in his way, attained a kind of wisdom? He did not seem surprised to see me, and asked me to come in. The room, probably used as a kitchen, judging from the smell of spice and olive oil, was in total darkness. A faint, strangely golden light was coming from the next room, lighting up his beautiful, smiling, friendly, serious face. He asked me to follow him. His faltering steps made me think he was limping, until I realised the child was decked out with old priestly vestments which got in his way as he walked. The golden light was coming from a paraffin lamp in a room laid out as a little indoor chapel, where the hermit was getting ready for the night service in front of a rustic, shining iconostasis. His shoulders now covered with a pink and green chasuble that was faded and threadbare with age, its fringe fraying, he gave me a discourteous glance and took no more notice of me. Censer in hand he began his litanies, repeated softly by the child, who was obviously the son of a mule-driver, an orphan delighted with his position as the servant of a hermit. They lit candles, murmuring a sacred, very ancient and very venerable text. The solitary opened a book, and in a very deep, cracked voice he sang a bizarre *melopoeia*, old as the sky and very sad.

Both of them seemed to have forgotten I was there, fascinated as they were by the browned gold of the icons. They bowed low before their humble Deësis, they anointed each other with incense, then, candles in hand, they swiftly recited the extremely long list of all the saints in Paradise, the boy, always one name behind, yelling Dimitrius, Pachomius, Gregorius, while the man was already at Saint John Chrysostom! Again they bowed before the icons; the boy lit a gold lamp with a wax taper. As he did so, he sang a canticle that must have dated back to the glory of Byzantium, and which, bastardized through the centuries, and sung in a nasal tone, was now no more than a raucous, savage song in his mouth. It echoed strangely in this little house, lost in the gorges of Athos. The celebration continued; they did not seem to get tired; they had gone into a trance; the boy was staring vacantly, and there was a wonderful beauty to his face; the monk bellowed, a little bell tinkled insistently, the censer answering it with its own ringing noise. Chant followed chant, petitions, incantations.

Now they were reciting the list of all the pious anchorites, confessors, virgins, martyrs, witnesses and doctors of the Most Holy Orthodoxy. The bell, rung by the boy, tinkled frantically: they were all set to evoke the Spirits until three o'clock in the morning in that fiery, candle-lit room, in that little chapel with walls of mud and straw painted scarlet. The candles and the lamps gave off an intense heat. The air, heavy with the smell of incense and wax, was intoxicating; the brilliance of all the gold fascinated me as well. The chants, whose great age took me back to the first nights on earth, were delirious and often exquisitely tender, and they made me drunk with pleasure. The boy danced from one foot to the other; the burning tallow was running down his fingers without him noticing. The anchorite, quickly gathering the folds of his many-coloured chasuble in front of him, made a deep bow almost to the floor, then suddenly knelt down, kissed the ground and stood up again, thundering out a new chant, his eyes closed, his face wild, his hair in disarray. Like them I was dancing from one foot to the other, my eyes closed. Then abruptly the festival ended with a last tinkle of the bell.

The hermit and his young acolyte came round, blew out the candles and shifted almost automatically from the sacred to the profane. He took off his pink and green chasuble, hung it in a cupboard and helped the boy get out of his finery. He carried the paraffin lamp into the kitchen, took a cigarette from his pocket, and lit it with the flame, nearly setting light to his tousled beard. He took a few puffs and finally seemed to remember I was there. Taking the lamp from the stove, he pushed open a door leading to a charming little bedroom whose open window looked out on to the cool river. He hung the lamp on a nail, and left without any further ado. I turned back the wick and put it out, and soon fell asleep on a narrow little bed whose pillows were stuffed with scented, sleep-inducing herbs.

I woke late. The mist had long since cleared. A hot sun shone down on the forest. A cloud of steam rose from the rushing stream, wetting the greenery of the deep gorge. I went through the dark, smoke-blackened kitchen, cluttered with cauldrons. I washed my face and joined them under an arbour, on a seat where I was given coffee. They wanted to know who I was, why I had come to the Sacred Forest. And so the discussions began. The boy could not take his eyes off me, smiling at me; as for the hermit, if my arrival the night before had seemed a nuisance, this morning I was a distraction from the immense boredom that I had often noticed among the monks of Athos. But was he really a hermit? His house was only one *skete* among many others, more basic perhaps, very isolated in the jungle. I was sure there was a truly solitary man higher up in the forest. They did not know of any. I persisted; they said it was true there were ancient caves further along in the cliffs, but it was well-known that they had been abandoned since the beginning of the century. I had an idea: to set myself up in a cave that was still habitable and, since I had lost hope of finding a master, to attempt the great adventure of solitary meditation alone, by becoming an anchorite myself. A wise man did live higher up in the forest: it was me, later on—for time is only an illusion. The good thing about Athos is that everyone is free to follow his own path. It is a tradition unchanged since Byzantium: go where you will, God will help you! I could have expressed the intention to live in a tree, to wear leaves and eat grass, without arousing the slightest surprise. Not only did my plan not surprise them, they even offered to show me how to get to the ancient caves straight away. Despite the heat, which was already strong, they were ready to leave right that minute, like all those who basically have nothing to do, and who are always ready to go for a walk in the woods; and also because, in the Land of the Spirits, what must happen is set in motion with the greatest of ease. Since arriving on Athos, my wishes had been granted almost instantly; each time I was surprised, charmed, delighted by it. I could not get used to the enchantments of the Holy Mountain. Here everything seemed very easy, and indeed it was, in a vast, uncertain time, constantly fragmented, unknown to humans.

I was given a glass of water … The sporadic cacophony of the cicadas sometimes became more insistent between moments of silence, during which everything seemed to be suspended, completely immobile. In the wild forest the cicadas were silent. I sensed a break in the flow of time; there was a divine moment of absolute existence, sufficient unto itself. Then everything began to move again. The sound of the nearby river, which flowed with a soft murmuring of fresh water as it washed over the rocks, came back to me. The cicadas sang, and I drank the glass of ice-cold water which had been put in front of me I knew not how long ago.

One point had yet to be settled however; it was broached discreetly, but firmly: did I have the parchment that the Great Ancients gave to those who are worthy of staying more than a few days on the Holy Mountain? I got out the parchment and handed it to him. He put on his glasses and read the text attentively from beginning to end. It was a long Byzantine text that I had never managed to decipher. He gave it back to me respectfully, with a most religious gesture of amazement: I was one of those who could live eternally on Athos! He all but kissed my feet! Out of modesty I hid them under the bench. I did not conceal from my hosts my emotion on hearing this decision by the Great Ancients, so rarely granted. Practically never, he exclaimed. The boy gazed at me in admiration. What is more, those who rule in Kariés had commanded that help and assistance were to be given to me unreservedly in these woods that I loved, to be happier than anyone could ever hope for, and to know that it was for always! This blank cheque giving me the right to live eternally on Athos … it didn't matter how accustomed I was to joy, that delicious moment when I learnt that I was saved for ever!

But who was it who was to live on in this incredible land? I asked if there was a name on the parchment. He took back the text that I was holding and read it out syllable by syllable: FRAN ÇOIS AU GI É RAS, he spelt, not without difficulty. The syllables rang out in the calm air, but meant nothing to anybody. The bees buzzed, a bird settled on a branch. It was probably my last incarnation. It was my eternal soul, indifferent to all notion of identity, which rejoiced in its survival … on a June morning, in a gorge on Athos.

In the shade of an arbour with a few cups of Greek coffee, I closed my eyes with happiness. For a while I no longer heard the song of the cicadas, nor the flight of the bees, nor the babble of the stream … I opened my eyes: I was being reminded about my plan to go and live in a cave. While the cicadas ceaselessly repeated their cry, the monk was already locking his door with a sharp turn of the key. He gave it a thump to make sure it was secure, then picked up a heavy staff. As for the child, he left empty-handed, cheerfully going on ahead of us along the path which, halfway up the rocks, climbed back up the stream.

We passed beehives made of plaited willow, covered with flat stones and planks, set up at the entrance to sad little caves where hay, tools, bundles of firewood, casks had been piled up; cool black caverns where, through the ages, other solitary men before them had put their barrels, rakes and forks in the Sacred Forest. We went through an undergrowth of young chestnut trees on a dangerous overhang, twenty-five metres above the water. The path became a narrow ledge; there was a way through but it was difficult, with a sheer drop to the river below. Suddenly I saw enormous caves, some roughly converted a long time ago.

In this part of Athos, everything was witness to a thousand years of occupation, works and signs that might have been older than Christianity. Stairs cut roughly out of the cliff, giant steps leading to rooms higher up, hollowed out by men: stone rooms with little openings like those in watch-towers, looking out at the jungle. At this point, worn-down and gently rounded by the water, enormous rocks that had once fallen from the cliff-top now blocked the river, which surged into a narrow channel with a noise like thunder.

One cave suited me: it was immediately decided that I would set up home there. They left me to explore the numerous passages that led back into cold darkness, and soon came back with a mattress, blankets and a paraffin lamp. I arranged a sort of camp for myself under a dry shelter on the fine, sandy ground. The boy ran to the hermitage and brought me a jumble of everything he thought would be useful. And so I inherited a small axe, a metal jug, a heavy cooking pot he had picked up in the woods, a candle, a can of paraffin and a little box full of incense. He put down his load in front of me, disappeared, and came back, out of breath, with new treasures that he piled up at my feet: a stool, some forks, a knife, a bolster and a short sword dating from the Ottoman occupation. As my setting up home in the holy caves caused him much childish excitement, he was gaily looting from his master to establish me comfortably in my new condition as a pious anchorite. This upheaval in the woods, in the full heat of the afternoon, and accompanied by the frenzied noise of the cicadas, amused and intoxicated him. Like all children who live alone with an old man, far from other men, he seemed a little mad, happy, very free. We watched him arrive with an alarm clock in one pocket and a chair in his hand. He apologised for being so poorly laden this time:

I dropped an eiderdown in the little wood, he laughed, and ran off to fetch it.

The sun was going down over the forest. It was time to leave me. The monk gave me a box of matches, and asked me to use them sparingly, for he did not have many at the moment. The respectful admiration he had shown that morning had quite disappeared. Was he really so overjoyed to have me as a neighbour? I knew this kind of man, simple and crude, with an utterly unstable temper, devoted one minute, almost aggressive the next; one of those very limited, very Christian people, devoid of courtesy, who being nothing, derive vanity from their solid rusticity; one of those people who, because they have been congratulated once on their plain speaking, believe they have the authority for the entirety of life to say all the stupid things that pass through their heads. He seemed furious at having enabled me to set myself up in the ancient caves. If it hadn't been for the blank cheque granted to me, perhaps hastily … by the Great Ancients of Kariés, the good man would have asked me to move on—a peasant, suddenly offensive, in a hurry to leave. It is true the wretch had reason to be annoyed, since the child had performed a veritable house-moving, going all out to loot his hermitage, chair and stool included, probably HIS chair and HIS only stool, for the benefit of a young stranger whose saintliness was in no way apparent.

"Every evening, when it is cool, the child will bring YOU coffee and vegetables."

He invested this "YOU" with all the coolness of one who hated strangers, and with a private satisfaction at being merely a humble gardener, a worker for Christ, without education. The hostility of a simple man mattered little to me: I had HIS chair, HIS stool, HIS blankets, HIS forks, and almost already HIS servant! The boy seemed completely smitten with me. Among other reasons for liking each other, did we not share a taste for pillage? The child wanted to kiss my hand. His master took him back with a roughness that upset me. After a blessing, purely for the sake of appearances, I was left in my cave in the middle of the indescribable camp of a shipwrecked man, abandoned to his solitude in a jungle that was suddenly silent at sunset.

A bench seat, carved out of the rock, provided me with a bed, on which I laid out the mattress and the blankets. I took the short sword I had been given, the box of incense and the cooking pot outside onto a sort of rocky porch that rose above the lively waters. Dead branches, which had fallen from the top of the cliff, littered the ground. I snapped some of them; they broke with a cracking noise that was taken up by the echoes. I threw them down beside three stones arranged into the shape of a hearth; and I waited for night to come, sitting by a substantial supply of dried branches. The insects had ceased their cries, and I was getting so used to the roar of the river that I no longer heard it.

At nightfall I was alone in the woods for the first time since I crossed over into the world of the Spirits. If death is like a shipwreck, then this one, among so many other shipwrecks and so many other deaths which I remembered hazily, fulfilled all my desires. The caves were good and dry, the air warm and very still at this late hour, the rock warm beneath my bare feet. I was young in the land of happy souls. This short sword, this cooking pot, this chair … beside this primitive hearth, seemed to have been carried there, not so much by the boy as by the powerful undercurrent from my distant past. Beyond the gates of death, a nomad's camp was all I needed to make me happy, for I was a very old spirit. My solitude, far from weighing me down, brought me back to my true nature, which dated from the very first evenings of the world.

Night came slowly; the huge arc of the forest stood out dimly against the sky. The song of the frogs, like a note repeated from octave to octave, penetrated deeply into the growing darkness, as far as distant, lost pools in the jungle. At this call, presences came out of the undergrowth: the birds, now sleeping, let their simple dreams wander along the river-bank; the souls of the trees, an exquisite perfume, spread through the warm air. Motionless by the fire I had just lit, I knew I was loved, accepted by timid presences who were intrigued by my encampment on the rocks, and attracted by my fire. There was nothing in me that did not share wholeheartedly in the nocturnal enchantment: not a glimmer of Christianity. I was a soul who had stayed intact since prehistory. Bewitched by the fire, I felt a strange power being born in my heart: I was attracting forces. Charms, profoundly loving and as old as the world, the true food of the Spirits when night comes, came from the rocks, the birds and the trees, settled on my lips and entered into me.

Someone was walking through the unseen stream: other foods were coming to me by river. The child walked out of the darkness and appeared by the fire, soaked to the knees, holding a heavy wooden dish. He put it respectfully on the stones and sat down by the fire discreetly, but without hiding the joy he felt at seeing me again. I had watched him enough during the day to realise that under his master's stern eye he played the good acolyte, the humble servant, out of caution and constraint. But several times his overexcitement had made me certain that this was a mask hiding his true nature, which thirsted for caresses, very free and unchristian. Had he too passed more or less into savagery? The first time our eyes met he seemed to have known instinctively that I was another him, able to satisfy all his secret desires straight away, most of all the unfathomable need for tenderness in the arms of an adult which is common to all primitive adolescents. For my part, I was hungrier for him than for the plate of tomatoes he had brought me.

His sanctimonious old master must rarely caress him. The child wanted to lean against my thigh, but made do with brushing my bare feet discreetly—deliberately I was sure—as he casually laid twigs one by one on my glowing coals. I could barely make out his face in the dim glow of our dying fire, but his brown, gentle hand spoke for itself: the child arranged the twigs skilfully, putting into this simple act his immense desire for sensual pleasure, as well a promise of discretion and devotion to me. It was as if he was saying: see, I am at your service. Why do you hesitate to ask more of me in the depths of this moonless night? The twigs, prettily criss-crossed, suddenly burst into flames, lighting up his gentle face, his big dark eyes, his sensual, still boyish lips, his fresh throat. He was watching me intently, seemed to expect everything from me; then he lowered his eyes, deliberately concentrating on the fire, suddenly awkward, unsure whether I appreciated his advances. Besides, what did he want? He had no idea: to love, to be loved, not really knowing in what way. To get closer to me. He remained very cautious, on his guard; our shadows were silhouetted on the rock face. The twigs soon burnt away. As an excuse to stay, he put more small branches between my stones, blackened by the flames. The last few brands, which had almost gone out and were barely glowing, only lit up his hand, which was trembling slightly, his lovely hand, which I suddenly took in mine.

It was all he had been waiting for. I felt him quiver. His whole being was seized with a great abandonment, a delicious joy. Closing his eyes he put his head on my shoulder, without letting go of my hand, which he was gripping tightly enough to break. I stroked his face; the dying embers left us in growing darkness, very black at the edge of the cliff. A sharp piece of rock was sticking into his hip; he moved slightly, opened his eyes and smiled at me, then his eyelids closed and he leant even closer against my heart. We stayed like that for a long time in the still night. There was a good smell about him, coming from his bramble-torn clothes, from his hair full of dust and dead leaves, from his brown, unwashed skin, healthy and hot. Peaceful slow breathing swelled his young chest and lifted the rounded shoulder that I hugged gently with my arm.

I leant over his face. The touch of my lips plunged him into a half-sleep; he remained inert in my arms, savouring the joy of being loved, his breathing suspended and, almost by magic, going into a trance. As for me, I kept looking at his beautiful face: had I loved this child in the world of men? I was certain that passionate links had united us on the other side of existence. But which ones, in which century? He opened his eyes. Truly, I saw his simple soul emerge from the depths of the unfathomable happiness where it had been for so long. Reaching the surface, it brought a heavenly smile to his lips. Softly he said a few words, familiar words of total devotion to me, of grateful servitude:

"You aren't eating; your food's getting cold."

I held him more tightly. "I have already known you," I told him, not caring about the plate of tomatoes that was going cold on the stone.

He toyed idly with my short sword; then he used it to put out our last embers by covering them with ash, as if he now wanted a darker night to surround our joy.

I asked him why had he come through the water?

"Because the narrow track at the side of the cliff is dangerous at night when there's no moon," he replied. This child who had come out of the water intrigued me. It was quite clear that he was no stranger to me. So who was it I had lost in the water in another life? Who, beyond death, was coming back to me along the river-bed?

He remained in a sort of happy lethargy, eyes closed, lips trembling. I, too, felt as if I were outside myself.

"In another life, in another life … "

"You will find me again! That's what I promised you," he breathed. "And you have found me among the dead, because I love you!"

I felt dizzy. I was sure that a promise had been made in another life. And by some miracle it had been kept. For a moment I thought I caught sight of the place where I had heard that voice before and clasped that light shoulder which was trembling in my hand. Those who love each other see each other again in the land of the dead: I knew it, but did not believe it.

"I waited for you for a long time," he whispered.

With a tender passion he gave me his cool little lips, whose taste I had known for all eternity. Suddenly we were just one single being, ablaze with joy! Tears ran down our faces. Drunk with happiness, we stayed in each other's arms for a long time, in the midst of a whirlpool of light. A harmony, endlessly repeated, divine, beyond any audible music, carried us off into elation, cast our love up into the heavens, brought us back to our caves. It mingled with the roar of the river, with the darkness of the forest, letting us glimpse a few fragments of our previous lives, our past loves. More often it was not in any one place or time, sufficient unto itself at the motionless centre of a perpetual jet of flame. The spell vanished. We came to, still quivering with joy, and sweetly intoxicated.

He drew back his arms, which he had wrapped round my neck, took a cigarette from his pocket and gave it to me. I put it beside the ashes, on a stone which was still hot.

"I must go now, for the night service," he said, getting up reluctantly.

"I'll come along the stream with you … "

He gave our camp a last glance; he slid the short sword into his belt, and went ahead of me over the rocks that led down to the stream, which we entered, holding hands. Without straying too far from the bank, supporting ourselves on branches that jutted out above the dark shallow water, which was quite warm at this time of night, we set off slowly downstream. We moved blindly along the undergrowth, never letting go of a branch, except to take hold of another, yet in danger of losing our footing at each step on the loose pebbles beneath the fast current that slapped against our legs. On that night when the moon was low, was I dreaming about the Land of the Spirits? The top of the massive cliffs, covered with bushes, stood out against vast white clouds, whose brightness contrasted with the warm darkness of the deep gorge. We stopped. The strong steady current ran between our thighs and deafened us delightfully under the lattice of the branches. Bay trees blocked our way: with one hand he slowly drew the bright sword from its scabbard; I saw it flash in the shadows, that were full of the heady smell of sap and running water. He beat down several branches and we set off again beneath the big white clouds, which were now drifting away from the steep cliffs above the river.

Crickets were singing in the jungle. The darkness brought us together passionately in the depths of the undergrowth and the water. Out of love, and for fear of falling and losing each other, we kept our fingers clasped together. He guided me; his gentle hand grasped mine with an unswerving tenderness a little sadly; for downstream, a golden gleam was shining in the thickest part of the woods: a paraffin lamp stood in the doorway of his master's house. It was time for us to part. Did he slip deliberately, and hold on to me so as not to be carried away by the current? Soaked to the waist, he stretched out to get his breath back on a rock that just broke the surface of the water. I leant over him. Had he hurt himself as he fell on the stones? He undid his clothes, put his arms around my neck and pulled me towards him with the almost delirious frenzy of a young savage giving himself unreservedly. I climbed onto the rock and lay down against his lovely, half-undressed body. I caressed his bare wet hips, soft and round.

"I love you," he said softly.

"I love you too, and I have always known you," I said, closing my eyes.

He pressed himself against me even more tightly, amid the cry of the insects and the crash of the waves: for a moment at the height of our joy, I had only a feeling of utter stillness, happy drunkenness, lightness—in contrast with the weight and the constant movement of the water that rushed over our rock. When I opened my eyes, it was swiftly carrying downstream twigs, dead leaves and long white milky trails drawn from the depths of our entwined bodies; long trails of human sap which floated and danced on the waves, then disappeared into the darkness. Not daring to part, we stayed together for a long time, deeply moved, deliciously tired, his cool cheek pressed against my brow, our hearts still beating to the rhythm of love.

Exquisite scents of laurel and flowers came from the undergrowth; the movement of the water cradled us, our passion was now just tenderness. If I had kept my eyes tight shut at the height of our pleasure, now I opened them wide: our bright steel sword shone on the rock; the insects were still screeching in the jungle, and the big white clouds of night were sailing above the dark cliffs pierced by caves. In the land of happy souls, what better bed could I have wished for than this rock, ceaselessly washed by the water?

We had to part. I helped the boy back into the water. At the moment we separated it was him, with an impulse of innocent savagery, who embraced me with all his youthful strength, little-versed in the gestures of love, completely unselfconscious, but perhaps knowing by instinct that this wholly primeval confusion that drove him to simply imitate the passion I had shown for him, this primitive error, lay at the very heart of the secret laws of the jungle. He soon loosened his naive embrace, not wanting to delay any longer. One last time his beautiful eyes gazed at me passionately. He squeezed my hand, gave me the sword, going from one extreme to the other, he offered me his lips with such sweetness, with such discreet modesty, that the subtlest perfumes of the forest were as nothing beside it. He promised to come back to my cave, and then disappeared into the shadows, wading along the river-bed.

Dreamy and enchanted, I stayed for a long time in the place where he left me. Completely satiated with him, I hesitated to go back. Some of his presence was still on my face, my clothes, on my hands. The strength of his love for me did not dissolve, but lingered deliciously here, where he had walked away from me.

Downstream, the paraffin lamp was taken from the doorstep; the leaves and the rocks returned to their peaceful darkness. I thought I heard songs, the sound of bells: they must be beginning their night office. The cold of the water was penetrating right into me, and I headed slowly back up to the cave. I retraced the course of our happy love, here and there gleaning the most lovely memories, taking hold of a branch which we had held, walking under bay trees where we had stopped, past a tree he had leant against, where I pressed my lips. Back in the cave, exhausted by exquisite tiredness, moved to my very soul, drunk, I sat down by the ashes of the fire. I laid my hand on them gently: they were soft and warm like the child, like the night. By chance, my fingers came across the cigarette he had taken from his pocket, his humble gift left on a stone. I had no desire to smoke, I had no desire for anything; I was fulfilled beyond all expectations, and was still imagining that I held the child to my heart, this child who had passed over into savagery, this part of me I loved, who loved me, and who I had found once more in the land of the dead.

I woke in the ancient caves. There are places so sanctified by the lives of those who lived there, that the mere fact of staying there, if only for a few hours, has the effect of calming the mind and making it more sensitive than usual. The cool rock was still permeated with a beautiful smell of incense, and the murmur of prayer seemed only recently to have ceased. A century? Compared with the most holy eternity it was only yesterday! In these sacred refuges, once inhabited by hermits, I felt welcomed by benevolent, peaceful forces which had watched me, judged me, and sounded me to my core.

They were hailing my arrival among the dead: they were rejoicing at my return to the land of happy souls. I had been known for centuries on this side of life! In return I greeted these venerable good Spirits, very old and wise. Until now I had met only pious, narrow-minded monks, whose crude words had saddened me. I thanked the Spirits of the holy caves for showing me a quite different language. I asked about the child. Being collective, the Spirits who lived in the caves answered me unanimously, with kindness and affection, that this love was right and praiseworthy. Having loved this child for centuries, I must inevitably see him again in the after-life. This joy belonged to both of us, for the child too had known me since the beginning of the world. I had the feeling that they were whispering to me that we were one single being; and I was also sure that great secrets would be revealed to me when I passed over the final thresholds, which still lay far ahead of me. But for the moment, scarcely dead, still dreamy, I should make the most of my joy before facing harsh ordeals.

I accepted enthusiastically the joys and sorrows that were always even-handed in the Land of the Spirits, where nothing really surprised me, unlike the affairs of men, whose anarchy was still an enigma.

Here at these beautiful caves, everything was equilibrium, peace, harmony and … silence, for I did not hear the rumbling of the river unless I thought about it. Leaving the rocky shelf where I had my camp, I went down some steps to a pool.

Getting undressed, I washed in pure water. I was still in something like a state of grace; I could still feel the presence of the ancient souls, who were watching me with kindness: beyond the gates of death I was loved, known since the beginning of time. This age-old care for me made a change from my loneliness among men. At last myself, one by one I was rediscovering the acts of the sacred: I had had nothing to eat for two days, but was none the worse for it. Up to my waist in a cold pool cut out of the rock, once the pond of an old mill, I washed myself as one prays. Every gesture on that peaceful Athos morning was nothing but joy and tranquil participation in the harmony of the world. Slowly I got out of the clear water and dried myself on some large rocks, scorching hot to my bare skin.

The heat soon forced me back into the shade of the cliffs. My dish of tomatoes, now covered in ants, was still on a stone; hunger really did not bother me; I was fed by my joy at living in the sight of the holy souls who roamed the caves and welcomed me with a very deep, quiet goodness that the world of men has lost for ever.

I leant my forehead on the dry rock, which was full of kindness for me: out in the jungle, the shrill cry of the cicadas was muted. I put my clothes on and sat in my humble campsite. The state of happy lightness in which I had woken was lasting a long time. The certainty of being watched, protected, gave me a feeling of security I had never had before. I felt loved by ancient Spirits of boundless wisdom. That morning, so blue and so clear, I asked myself what was going to happen to me. The immediate reply was that I had to wait before what I wished for most of all came true: before dying to myself in the second death, I must use up the final joys that were owed to me. Although they were rather crude, they were the consequence of my actions, and more so of my desires, accumulated through many lives.

Today, in the shade of the cliffs, in the land of echoes and the dead, I waited only for the child. I shut my eyes, opened them almost immediately, and saw him! He was coming back up along the bed of the stream. Was he the same, had he grown since the night before? I remembered a child of between thirteen and fourteen, but he appeared to be fifteen or sixteen! He walked delightfully through the water. His movements were beautiful, his bearing rather like a dancer. So where had I seen this handsome adolescent before? And what is love, if not a profound memory, both of the other person and of yourself?

A straw hat, a switch in his hand, a linen jacket thrown gracefully over his slim shoulder, he smiled at me a little awkwardly at the memory of our caresses and the thought that his arrival, so early in the morning, showed that he wanted more. He climbed some steps in the bank and, without a word, sat down discreetly on the rocky ledge where I had set up camp. He brought me his presence: from me he expected the affection and the boldness that he was hoping for. I joined in his game. I pretended not to notice he had arrived, sifting through my ashes, taking out a few coals that could be used again. My fingers soon met a soft brown hand, permitted to stray so close to my stones that I could not help but brush it in passing, a delightful, friendly hand, open like a flower, which shuddered with pleasure at my first caress, then throbbed when I gripped it tightly.

We stayed like that, holding hands, for a long time without saying anything. I felt he was still timid; I questioned him, if only to distract him from his shyness, and to give me an excuse to keep his hand in mine without him withdrawing it out of modesty.

I asked him his name, suddenly remembering that all notions of identity are just an illusion. So who was it who was standing beside me? Was I even sure that the child of today was the same as yesterday? He replied that he was called Joshua. He was dead and knew it, without quite believing it. I looked at his lifeline. It was very short, that of a boy who had died very young. Our fingers entwined again, more closely, more lovingly. Was he the son of a mule-driver, or a sailor? He had an eagerness for pleasure about him, very much the mule-driver, mixed with a grace in his ever-so-slow, precise movements, something that is only learnt at sea, to the rhythm of the swell. It appeared that he had not known his parents, only an uncle, a fisherman who sometimes took him out in his boat. After several years in an orphanage he had found himself back with the monks of Athos. His slight memory did not go beyond the recollection of mown grass and working in the garden. He loved listening to the birds singing, throwing stones in the stream, bathing in the sea. He did not complain about his master, who was strict with him but rarely beat him. He turned his beautiful face towards me, blushing delightfully.

"I was waiting for you," he said.

The truth was, this Helladic child, fisherman's son or not, belonged only to the world of the sacred. I had seen him already, on icons, miniatures and frescoes, in David, in the child Abraham guarding his father's flocks. Joshua belonged only to the world of monks and painters: another world, freer, happier than that of men who are merely men locked in the infernal cycle of birth and procreation. Joshua seemed very old. These kind features, this strong, supple body, with rather thick ankles, this quiet nature, not the least narrow-minded, but simple, dated back to Byzantium, and came from the islands and the Eastern Mediterranean. With the soul of a servant, yet devoid of servility, affectionate and discreet, wanting caresses, little interested in women, he seemed to have always lived among hermits and icon-painters, as a disciple, almost a slave, devoted through love. Had I known Joshua in those distant times when people knew that it is the adolescent boy who is beautiful, divine, worthy of love, more deserving than women of inspiring desire and attachment—those days when adolescent boys knew it too; and when mortals could still remember young angels sometimes visiting the wisest humans? I could clearly see Joshua in the little studios of the Byzantine painters, built onto the sides of monasteries, crushing up the paints, cooking the supper: Joshua through the ages, and myself with him. The depth of my love for this child had no other reason than my incredible memory.

He noticed the plate of tomatoes which I had not touched.

"Not eating?" he said in a charming voice.

"I am hungry for you!" I replied.

He got up slowly, calmly, and, since I was hungry for him he suggested I follow him upstream. Wisely, he did not want to risk being caught by his master in a cave with me; no doubt he also wanted to take a walk higher up in the jungle. This caution and a taste for wandering were two traits of my own character. Discovering them in Joshua made me love him even more, and want to embrace him even quicker. We soon left the river, whose strong current was getting dangerous, and climbed beautiful meadows that sloped gently under the blue summer sky, wild meadows with black pines towering over them. We were high up; the air was bright, light, crystal clear, and smelt of resin. Sparrow-hawks hovered overhead. More slopes and a track brought us back to the cold water. Upstream of my cave, old windmills and abandoned barns rotted from one season to the next.

Under an overhang of cliff was something almost like a village, with its courtyards, stables, roofs of grey, mossy stone pierced by odd little triangular skylights. There were enormous Byzantine stables of incredible beauty, made of pink brick with narrow windows. On the upper floors, hoists had once been used to haul up forage and wheat; chains and rusted pulleys still hung there. In the cold shade of the rock, nettles and brambles were growing everywhere; the sun never entered these courtyards where our love for each other was growing stronger by the minute. Dragged from their slumber by the sound of our footsteps on the damp green flagstones, the souls of mule-drivers and sturdy blacksmiths urged us on to pleasure, and lived again in us. Simple souls, deprived of pleasure for centuries. Hence our impatience to find a safe hiding place. It was as if we were expected, and lured in. Were they souls? More like ancient desires which still impregnated the walls. A long shaky ladder that was leaning against the rock led to an old loft made of daub and planks. Joshua climbed up the weak dangerous rungs and I followed. On that clear, divine morning as we slowly got higher above the stone roofs and the dancing reflections of the river and the roar of the water, sometimes feeling giddy on the unsafe ladder, we got to a loft in semi-darkness, and filled with hay right up to its many beams, between which came a few shafts of light. It was wonderfully constructed, like a basketwork of dead trees and struts, interwoven, pegged together, giving the feeling that this was nothing less than a storeroom for dreams, a vast memory, a mysterious undergrowth into which we crawled.

Here we saw little rooms for grooms, with flimsy partitions made of dried earth, poor rooms also full of hay, their tiny windows giving glimpses of blue sky. Dirty jackets and cloves of garlic still hung on nails. A strong smell of forage and dung went to your head. Bees buzzed. Joshua lay down in the dry grass, and I propped myself up on my elbows beside him.

Was it his joy to be alone with me in this haunted loft?

He seemed more handsome every minute, more desirable. His face was slightly flushed with tiredness; his half-open shirt revealed a drop of sweat on his young chest. He watched me in silence. Who was I in his eyes? Another him, older, freer, more educated, while I saw in him the adolescent part of my eternal soul. Had I been Joshua in Byzantium, in the East, on the islands? Was it from him that I had got my mule-driver's tastes and some of my country manners? Everything drew me to this fifteen-year-old boy, his lovely body, his nature. Our hands met. There was a discreet modesty about him, a simple nobility. For a long time his fingers lay still in mine. However much I caressed his hand more deeply and more deliciously, it ignored my appeal. Time passed. Joshua stood up to my gaze and continued to watch me. I was overcome with sadness. At last he remembered that he had known me for all eternity … very slowly his hand closed round mine in a warm, sweet embrace, which plunged me into perfect happiness! He closed his eyes: among all the possible caresses, he seemed to be waiting for the very ones I wanted to give him. This similarity in our natures filled me with desire as much as it reassured me. With someone so close, so brotherly, so like myself, a lack of fear filled me with great affection for him, which became attraction.

"I love you," he said softly.

I bent over his wonderfully beautiful face. With that exquisite gravity that only boys have, he gave me his lips and his soul to kiss, his soul, as fresh as the river's roar. In a big bed of hay, we kept our lips pressed together for a long time. Our kisses were sweet; he put all his heart into them, as did I. An old spell came from him; Joshua smelt of the sheepfold, the stable. With one hand he unbuttoned his trousers, made of coarse blue cloth; he bared his hips, a little feminine, round and white. Our pleasures over, we stayed in each other's arms, deeply moved, covered in sweat, our clothes dishevelled. I pressed my forehead against his child's cheek, I breathed in the breath from his lips. Drunk with pleasure, he fell asleep in the hay. A breeze, slipping in through the stone roof, brought us its coolness. I opened my eyes for a moment, long enough to glimpse the blue sky between the gap in two stones, a morning blue, the colour of our love. Reflections from the stream came through the skylights and danced on the beams. I closed my eyes again, in a hurry to return to our joy, so profound that it dazed me.

When I came to he was already getting up, doing up his clothes. I did likewise. We could have stayed longer, but we were in a hurry to leave each other. We climbed down from the loft and went back to the cave.

A full coffee pot had been put on a stone. So, his master had come to our camp while we were in the hayloft.

Joshua left in a hurry, rather nervous about the reception that awaited him at home. He held out his hand, as if to say: I haven't finished my day's work yet. Because of you, I'm going to get the rod!

The noonday heat forced me to find some shade. I sat on the chair, whose unexpected presence in my little cave was due to Joshua's kindness. I was falling asleep to the deep note of the cicadas when I thought I heard cries … I did not worry, knowing he was strong enough to take a good thrashing, and of a nature to enjoy it.

The sky was grey, heavy. Over the jungle, a summer storm rumbled in the distance. Late in the afternoon, still drowsy from my snooze, I was very glad to drink his master's delicious cold coffee. I was still sleepy, outside of myself, not quite remembering what I was doing in these woods. Making the most of this state of absence, my phenomenal memory dived into the past like a swimmer who lets himself sink. I was certain of it: I had lived in these caves around 1750. It was not such an ancient era. I often thought I had lived on Athos when the Byzantine galleys put in at its ports; it was true that some of my memories dated from the eighteenth century—almost yesterday.

I returned to the present. The storm was approaching. I only had time to bring in the dry wood and my box of incense before the first showers were followed by pattering rain, which flooded the ashes and scattered my campsite. The forest disappeared under a downpour. For a whole hour I stayed in my refuge, frightened, deafened by the explosions of the lightning and the muffled roar of thunder which was repeated by the echoes of the caves. Trees collapsed. Long electric streaks dropped from the black sky with a sound like fabric being slowly torn. The storm went away, came back, and crashed down on the woods and the rocks, lighting up the jungle with its blinding flashes. A violent, heavy rain whipped the muddy river, red with clay torn from its banks; tossed up into short waves, it swept away branches and rushed downstream. Torrents of rain, cascading from the top of the cliffs, bounced off the rocks, then poured into the raging flood; left on a stone, my wooden plate was carried off and thrown into the stream, where it drifted off, bobbed up and down on the swirling water, and sank. The rain stopped, the storm went quiet. The clouds tore themselves apart, revealing the blue sky. A great silence fell over the newly-washed jungle, ravaged and very green under a new sky.

I still had some dry wood. I lit a fire in the entrance to the cave. Once I had glowing embers I threw on some incense. A bird sang in the trees. Large drops of water were still falling from the cliff and splashed in front of me on the rocky ledge where nothing remained of my poor encampment. I closed my eyes: the perfume of the incense mingled with the smell of the damp earth, with the scent of the cedars and the bay trees with their black trunks. I withdrew into myself once more, full of gratitude and love for the kindly, peaceful forces that protected me in the holy caves.

During the first days of death, the absence of God comes as a surprise. Was I dreaming before actually dying? Did I want to pass through the final thresholds that separated me from the Clear Primordial Light? The Spirits replied that I was indeed dreaming; I was in Devakhan, the land of happy souls who do not yet see God. A vast dream, born of my desires, my tendencies and from the undercurrent of my past, was holding me in its spell! I could stay for a long time in this delightful state, or move on towards the Light by waking from my own death.

But who was I? My question made the good wise Spirits smile. I got an answer: that THAT WHICH survives is NAMELESS, for it is merely the temporary consciousness of sensations, experiences and ideas that come from past lives, as much as from the probable direction of future lives. If I wanted proof of this, my wanderings in the beyond quite obviously belonged to me, and made me very happy without me even knowing who I was! For was it not a fact that, not without some surprise, I was managing very well without knowing who was sitting at the entrance to a cool cave, watching night fall. The fact that my virtues and my faults were intact, still alive on this side of life, was more important to me than a name: if the first passer-by had my exact character, I would have gladly exclaimed that he was me for a while.

We returned gently to my vague desire to cross the final thresholds. It was my right to remain in Devakhan, to set myself up in these caves, to see the child every day. My past was known; I was an old dreamer, so much so that I ran the risk of never awakening. Dead, my faculties for dreaming were increased tenfold; I was going to dream for a thousand years and then be reincarnated. The thought of returning one day to the world of men frightened me so much that I begged the Spirits to help me pass through all the thresholds they wished. I could expect no help: IT WAS UP TO ME TO AWAKEN MYSELF! However, they took note of my decision to emerge from a great dream. I must give up the enormous share of joy that was still owing to me, and die the second death. Certain Spirits, who had loved me for a long time, promised me their discreet assistance; no more could be done for me. At which point I stretched out on my blankets and, utterly exhausted, fell asleep almost immediately.

At dawn I took a walk along the rocks. Having set off in search of a master, I found myself alone again. My master was myself! I wished to awaken but was incapable of doing it; I wanted to see the sea again, the beaches. The innkeeper's prediction came back to me: we will see you again soon in Kariés. I continued to dream, only this time I knew I was doing it. Solitude weighed heavily on me. I was beginning to tire of myself and of the consequences of my past actions, as one tires of many echoes that are only entertaining for a moment.

In the high jungle I thought I heard my name: a brother soul was asking me for help. Scarcely dead, it was wandering. Ancient bonds, a debt of gratitude, united me to this soul. It dared not set sail for the Holy Mountain; still very young, timid, knowing nothing of the Land of the Spirits, it was not like me, accustomed for centuries to being born and dying. I decided to answer this call immediately: I loved this soul! And I wanted to bathe in the sea.

So I got ready to leave, in a hurry to go to this dead soul who I sensed was somewhere near Ierissos, wandering on the shore and not daring to take a boat for Athos. I tidied up my extraordinary camp; I left my chair, my blankets, my box of incense and my cooking pot in the little cave. I thanked the Spirits for their kindness. They gave me to understand that I was nothing but an incorrigible vagrant. I promised to come back. Was I wrong to go to this soul? After a long silence … born out of vast, deep time, constantly in danger of breaking apart, disjointed, peculiar to this region of the beyond … or because my consciousness was in the process of being destroyed … I got the reply that I must indeed discharge myself from this final debt. They would await my return: sooner or later in this wild gorge, I would move on to the AWAKENING.

Reassured by this, and delighted to be hurrying to the sea, I set off cheerfully along the river-bed. It promised to be a scorching hot summer day. Even at this early hour of the morning, I had to look for cool shadows that the overhang of the cliff threw here and there on the water. I met Joshua washing a saucepan in a tranquil pool.

Quietly we said a few words to each other: I was sorry he had been beaten because of me. Poor Joshua! To my amazement he said that no one had beaten anyone in these woods yesterday … His master had simply asked him to spend less time with me. But I was sure I had heard howling! Where did it come from? What echoes of a hearty thrashing, lost for centuries, had reached my cave yesterday? Whatever the case, it was best for us to separate for a while, for caution's sake. Still, he was upset that I was going. He made me promise to come back quickly. Everyone here would certainly be looking forward to my return—except his old master, who I glimpsed saying his rosary on his flowery balcony, and who was relieved to see me leave.

In a hurry to get to Kariés I went quickly, still walking in the river, which was more passable than the Jungle of Snakes. Then I entered the forest of millennial cedars. I found the mule-drivers' tracks again, the narrow paths beneath the branches leading to mysterious forest rides closed off by long beams, intertwined with the skill and ancient wisdom so characteristic of the monks of Athos. I had long since left the Sacred Forest when I saw the roofs of Koutloumousiou and the gardens of Kariés.

I climbed the hundred steps that led up to the first alley-way. Doors were shut and everyone was asleep in the oppressive heat. I avoided my inn and headed for another one, built of blue wooden planks in the shade of an arbour. I was starving, and had pockets full of money. I ordered a lavish meal. I stuffed myself with meat, plates full of vegetables, delicious kebabs and wine, then fell asleep leaning on the table. Around four in the afternoon I was woken by the murmur of vespers in a nearby church. It was time to go. Dazed by the heat, I went across Kariés and took the tracks that led down to the beaches, dancing with joy at the thought of seeing the foaming waves again, the battlemented towers and the icon-filled monasteries of this land without women.

I felt at home: so much so that on impulse I had bought a monk's habit in Kariés. I was eager to put it on, and as I went through the woods I laughed to think that the money from the sale of a Luftwaffe uniform was now letting me impersonate a young and pious novice! My bundle under my arm, I spotted the sea, very blue, very calm, a lovely sight between the green trees.

My steps rang out under a cool arch. I entered the courtyard of Iviron. On Athos I went from surprise to surprise, without being surprised by anything any more, and even taking pleasure in the expectation of new enchantments. I remembered Iviron, where I had landed on the first morning of my death, as a large, rather poor monastery where I had had great difficulty in getting some food. This time, by contrast, I was asked to please come up to a small drawing room, very religious, with old lithographs on the walls, and furnished with divans and pretty pedestal tables. They brought me coffee and cigarettes; I was promised an excellent supper. Tired after my long walk, I let myself be carried along by this new enchantment. I put my cup and my packet of cigarettes on the stone sill of a window protected by rusty bars, through which I could see the jungle. They gave me a heavy notebook bound in black cloth, in which travellers put their names, their signatures.

It was the first time I had seen this register. When I came to Iviron a few days before, I no doubt appeared so poor that they had not even asked who I was. I had not forgotten that I was in search of a soul: had it already arrived here? I did not know the name of this dead person. I flicked through the book at random, convinced that a recent signature would most likely be his. To no avail: he must still be in Ierissos. To amuse myself I went through the previous years ... suddenly I recognised my name, my signature! In 1952 a François Augiéras had passed through Iviron! It was now 1954: a François Augiéras completely unknown to me! My head spun. Quickly I flicked through the years '50-'51. In June '51 an Augiéras had slept at Iviron! For several years, another me had been walking on Athos!

Dreamily, I put the register on the window sill: I thought I was lost! Who then, in the calm of the evening ... had his face pressed against an iron bar, listening to the singing of a spring whose fresh water ran in a walled kitchen garden? I had to know nothing about it and remain a stranger to myself. I was dead, and had forgotten it! After a moment's panic, I felt a deep, almost savage joy. So what did I have to complain about? The fragmentation of time gave me a feeling of lightness, of taking a holiday on the shores of most holy eternity. The loss of some identity or other mattered little to me, since in the after-life the consequences of my past made me a still younger being, open to all pleasures and coming across them almost everywhere. This land of inexpressible beauty, the tinkling of the bells, time subtly altered by the nearness of the ETERNAL, fulfilled all my desires. This land without women: its divine aspect touched the depths of my soul; its shameless aspect, which was mostly concealed, pleased me more than I could say. On the Holy Mountain, where no two clocks told the same time, time was constantly destroyed, begun again, shattered. I was slowly getting used to it; it gave me a rest from life.

I felt protected, known all my life, since I no longer knew who I was. He who is no more, fed and housed for free! I was invited into a smoky little kitchen near the drawing room, and to sit on a bench seat where a young mule-driver was sitting. He quickly put his legs between mine. We were given soup and resinous wine. On that beautiful July evening I began to rejoice openly at being dead. They brought my bag, which I had lost. Where? I did not know. Somewhere on Athos. I always managed to find it again; for nothing is lost in the after-life, everything always comes back to you. The little sugar and instant coffee it still contained were welcome. I promised myself a delicious cold coffee in my room. Then I remembered I was leaving for Ierissos tomorrow: again I was going to have the pleasure of sailing. Ever since I set foot on Athos everything had gone well for me: the many pleasures were followed by even more! I went up to bed, more determined than ever not to return to the present century.

A boat left me by the beautiful meadows of the Bay of Bulls. With a little luck another boat, sailing past, would see my signals and take me on-board. If fate stayed on my side I might even reach Ierissos today, and hurry to this soul whose call I could hear.

Day rose over the smooth green water. Not an animal in sight. I walked for a while on the snow-white shingle. I stretched out on the stones. On my belt I had a metal flask. I made some coffee in a mug, which was also metal, and clinked when I put it down on the still-cold stones, soft to the touch, polished by the tide. When I had drunk the coffee I explored my surroundings, not straying too far from my bag, which I had dropped on the shore.

Alone and delighted to be so, I went into the meadows that stretched back from the beach. There was nothing but peace and divine tranquillity in these first hours of a hot clear summer day. I saw gently rounded hills, trees, parkland deserted by the herds.

A bellow shattered the silence! Above an open-air maze, two fine white horns were outlined against the line of hill-crests.

I went up to a drystone wall. A young bull with long eyelashes like a woman was standing stock-still at the far end of one of the fields. A black yearling, he was watching me calmly. Charming but still timid, already strong, with a gleaming coat, he was attractive. He was curious about my being on the wall, but it did not upset him. He was alone in his paddock, closed off by a heavy gate. There was love between the two of us. Did he guess that I understood his boredom, his desires?

Leaving the little wall where I had been leaning, I slipped slowly into his meadow. I got close enough to touch his damp pink muzzle. With one hoof he stamped the ground, which was covered in hoof-prints and scattered with dung and straw. He lowered his head, not to charge, but seemed to be waiting for a gesture, a caress. With one finger I stroked his low forehead, covered in white hair. His fine bright horns attracted me. I grabbed them with both hands. We tussled happily. I tried to push him onto the ground. He did his best to free himself from my grip by suddenly shaking his head hard enough to almost break my wrists. Panicking, dragging me to the ground, he fought fiercely. Our game was becoming a lovers' embrace. Despite his shying I kept hanging on to his horns; his hard hoofs threatened to hit me in the stomach any moment; I was feeding off his strength, his frenzy; his powerful smell made me drunk with pleasure; his saliva ran down my arms. He jammed me into a corner of the enclosure, up against a wall whose sharp stones tore my shoulders! Covered in blood, my arms hurting, nearly passing out, I let go, reluctant to give up the beautiful white horns.

He leapt aside and planted himself in the middle of the field, tail whipping his sweating sides, more frightened than angry. He was young and so was I. I got up, covered in dust, happy, delighted, my clothes torn. He stayed some distance away from me, still on his guard, afraid I might grab him by the horns again. Leaving him in peace, I climbed onto the wall again and got my breath back.

He watched me, trembling at my slightest move, but slowly calming down. He even came closer, almost in reach of my hands. I did not frighten him any more; he sought out my gaze, my presence. That morning, the most cheerful of my life, sitting on the wall of a maze, I would have talked to a young bull in the sweet language of friendship and love, had I not seen a sail.

A boat was coming round a headland. I ran to the beach. I was sure it had spotted me. But would they put in? As the boat went behind an island, I took advantage of the moment to open my bag and put on the monk's habit I bought in Kariés. Hurriedly I wrapped it round me; I drew it in at the waist with a good bit of rope; I put on my boots … The prow of the boat reappeared from behind the reefs.

What fisherman of Athos would have dared not take on-board a young monk waving his arms on a deserted shore? The tiller turned instantly, they nearly ran aground on the shingle. They were going to Ierissos, the same as this "young ecclesiastic".

Helm set for the open sea again, the sail hoisted and filled by the wind, I sat in the prow made of strong blue boards and could not stop myself laughing at my transformation; I loved the game, in it I saw the secret of life: to mislead, to change clothes, to be someone else for a while in order to live forever! And besides, the religious habit suited me well: the collar of my shirt wide-open at the neck, as was the custom of the monks of the Holy Mountain, the floating robe hitched up in front over my blue cotton trousers, barefoot in my boots, I saw myself as a handsome boy, rigged out this way! Not only that—on this happy day in July I was going to a friend, not a friend of the heart but a loyal companion in adventure, as far as I could place him in my former lives, which was hardly at all. I was dead and no longer forgot it. All that reached me were the last echoes of a past which was becoming foreign to me … final echoes from far away, like the clear green waves that boomed against the hull every now and then as they ran into our boat, then carried on, indifferent, towards the rocks ahead where they would be crushed.

Athos fell into the distance. We left the holy water, deep and cold, and entered a wide bay.

The beach at Ierissos was visible on the horizon. Ierissos; the gate to return to the present century, to the Land of Mortals. The broadly curving, feminine coast seemed very attractive and very beautiful, with its fields of yellow wheat sloping gently down to the sea. Children and horses were walking in the foam under the blue sky of Greece. The motion of the swell, which was making the boat rock, slowly lifted up this delightful landscape, which went out of sight, then appeared again above the side.

Engine stopped, sail down, we made our own headway; the stern was now slicing through the shallow water, silky and warm. A slow, voluptuous music, enough to make you want to be reincarnated in a woman's belly, came from a small café built of multicoloured planks on the brilliant white sand of the beach. The song of the *bouzoukis* was carried on the sea breeze, mingling its soft tones with the rhythm of the swell. A half-naked child drank lemonade in the shade of a roof made of reeds. Young girls cooled their beautiful brown thighs in the calm surf. At each breaking of the waves they lifted their light, bright dresses up to their waists—solemnly, peacefully; they were Greek, happy. I desired the girls! For the love of boys was only a progression for me, the refusal of a new incarnation. The keel of the boat touched the pebbles; we dropped anchor. The land where you die, or are born, however desirable it may seem, is an illusion that no longer had any hold over me. I had known other joys, the world beyond.

I wanted to take my friend there. I saw him, asleep in the shade of a caique drawn up on the shore. I went over and woke him with a touch of the shoulder. Opening his eyes he recognised me almost immediately, despite my religious get-up, which did not seem to surprise him. According to him I had been a cheerful type for all eternity! We fell into each other's arms. He had been wandering the beach for several days, hoping I would come. He was quite timid, and my arrival got him out of a predicament, for he did not dare sail to the Holy Mountain on his own.

Each person takes into death what matters most to him. He was loaded down with a heavy bundle, some saucepans, coils of rope, an axe, salt, spices, hooks and pepper wrapped up tightly in a sheet, for he was hoping to sleep on the beach, to fish, and be self-sufficient without asking for hospitality from the monks of Athos. We bought a few things; laden with cans of oil, sugar and bread we went back to the shore. Cheerful as I had rarely been, my mind off my solitude, well-supplied with provisions, delighted to go to sea again, I felt no regret as I watched Ierissos fade into the distance. We were going to live on the beaches, fish, and bathe. I was returning to the after-life, and not alone. Could I ask for any greater happiness?

His joy at sailing towards the white marble of Athos reminded me of the first morning of my death. The forests and the deserted shores of this divinely beautiful land, uninhabited by women, filled him with wonder, and amazed him.

Leaning on my elbows in the stern, rocked by a strong swell … did I guess that I was living my last happy days, that I was soon going to cross the thresholds that separated me from the AWAKENING; that terrible burns were destined to be the beginning of the end for me?

Had I glimpsed the culmination of a great dream, the destruction of my being? Did my eyes hope for a dream that did not have the deceitful colours of the sky and the water? I was soon to die the second death, and did not know it. And yet the dull thud of the swell striking the hull, echoing strangely, worried me. Today the waves were surging into the sea-caves with a force I had never seen! Their cascading jets of spray, the booming of the surf, the frenzy of the mad waves … shattered and deafened my soul. Everything in me was breaking apart, roaring with the wind. One by one the last links that tied me to life snapped cleanly, like weak moorings. The struggling of our wooden boat as it was manhandled by the sea, the merry thunder of the waves hitting the shore ... drowned out the cries, the moans of my soul which, without my knowing, was already freeing itself from me.

On the waves of a peaceful bay, everything calmed down. Sheltered from the wind, engine switched off, our caique slipped silently towards the shingle. We went ashore at Iviron. In the Land of the Spirits, through the meadows, we walked up to the monastery. It was early afternoon and a sultry heat came from the forests, noisy with the many cries of the insects. My wanderings continued, this time in the company of a brother spirit.

This friend from my likely past brought me out of my solitude; his affection touched me, and I returned it in full. It was good to hold his hand tightly in mine, to lean on his strong shoulder. And this joy was also owed to me. Yet I suspected that this final and powerful echo of my former lives was the forerunner of the great silence that heralded the Clear Primordial Light; this last, all-too-human bond, could only be soon to break. Although happy to see this old friend, did I already want him to leave? A great labour was going on in my heart: I was weary of knowing that I had lived. I was now becoming accustomed to being no more than a soul, close to the AWAKENING, disinterested in itself, more than half-destroyed, knowing it, and becoming frightened.

While I was having a nap in one of the cool little rooms of this old monastery, he set off along the rough paths that led up to Kariés. At the height of the heat, with the cicadas calling, he came back with a parchment giving him the right to live 'eternally' on the Holy Mountain! We danced with joy over this; I gave him some cold coffee to help him recover from his long walk in blazing sunshine. But was he going to stay with us for a long time? Wouldn't he soon return to the world of men, like most of the souls who are quite unable to get used to the other side of life?

He liked only the beaches: was he going to get to know nothing of Athos except the water? Everyone carries their own Paradise within them. His was a sea-going paradise: it drove him away from the ancient monasteries I loved, and so we travelled along the north coast in the hope of settling down, deep in some deserted creek.

Since the clear dawn, we had been walking along through the foam, carrying our heavy load of saucepans, supplies and rope. At a beach of very fine sand, shaped like an arc, something made us stop. I knew it; I had bathed here. Overlooking it from high above was a hill covered in broom and flowers. Sweet-smelling bushes came right down to the edge of the shingle. Bees were buzzing by the water, skimming over the surf, then flying back off into the many colours of the countryside.

We quickly pitched camp round some sandstone tables—held down by their weight alone, polished smooth by the years, soft to the touch, great divine blocks left there by the sea. We put the loaves on them. He set up our sheet to protect us from the sun. Using an arrangement of long stakes and fishing line, he stretched it out above the stones. The sea breeze swelled it gently; cool shadows were cast on the sand.

He was a sturdy lad of thirty, skin tanned by the sun, and silent by nature: I tried to remember him. He came from a long way away. He went back to the time of my youth, when the gods reigned over these shores. I lit a fire and fetched some wood, while he fished on the furthest reefs. He emerged from the sea, dripping with foam, fish hanging from his waist, carrying a basket full of sea urchins. He threw his catch on the sand; I washed them in the light swell. From a spring that he found further up the beach, he brought back my metal can full of fresh water.

We ate in the shade of the sheet, our eyes dazzled by the light, propped up on our elbows at our sandstone tables on the beautiful, bright sand, saying nothing, listening to the quiet song of the tide. The joy of seeing each other again made our hearts beat in our broad chests. I grabbed his hand and squeezed it tightly in mine, tightly enough to break it.

"I love you," I said, "with a pure, noble love."

He did not answer, but a smile full of friendship came to his lips. He poured me some resinous wine in a silver tumbler he had given me; then he asked me about the Holy Mountain. I told him about my incessant wandering, my incredible adventures. Was I inventing them? I assured him I was not! To hear me talk you would have thought I was a quite a braggart, more Greek than the Greeks, and a liar like no other! He treated me as Ulysses with a thousand tricks, a vagrant taken in by magic spells. I continued my story, surprised him, made him laugh. At noon, as the heat was getting unbearable, we sheltered under a large tree.

When night came, beside an enormous fire we lit on the beach, I finished telling him about my many wanderings, each word, each phrase gently given rhythm by the steady sound of the surf which echoed in the shadows. I fell silent; a wave broke on unseen pebbles. Did he still see me as a friend? Or more of a magician in the firelight?

I told him about THE ADVENTURES OF THE SOUL, Daughter of the Light: her countless incarnations from age to age and from mask to mask; her return to the Land of the Spirits after each death, but only for a time; a delightful or unbearable stay, in fair reward for her actions and especially for her tendencies. The chance for some souls to never be reincarnated again, as long as they crossed the thresholds that lead to the AWAKENING: as long as they agreed to die the second death, the final ordeal leading to the Clear Primordial Light. If not, after a varying period of happiness or horror, sometimes a long dream, comes the inevitable return to the world of men.

In the warm night full of stars, on that deserted beach, he asked if I wanted to return to the world of men. I replied that I had come too close to the AWAKENING to wish to see mortals again. Even if I wanted to it was now too late. I had reached a point of no return, beyond which I could only head towards the light. Such was my destiny, which I gladly accepted; my voice was now no more than an incantation, half-sung beneath the bright stars of the Holy Mountain: soon I would to die to myself and to my own dreams … and I knew it.

In the darkness, his hand found mine and squeezed it very tight, as you hold the hand of a wounded man who you know is going to die. So who had I been in my many lives? And where had I met this brother spirit? Did he remember me, my last incarnation? He remembered me … and did not want to tell me anything, as you avoid tiring a dying man. The pressure of his hand on mine just got stronger, more friendly, in memory of our adventures in the world of men. Since this very old friend knew me like a brother … had I been a noble and courageous spirit, despite all my faults? On the warm sand the pressure of his hand got even stronger—out of a sort of respect and affection for me—and seemed to answer my final question passionately, and with a yes.

Our embers had long since gone out, leaving us in peaceful darkness. I had thought I was rushing to a soul in distress, but in fact it did not need any help; on the contrary, it was me, lost in solitude, who it had come to comfort. Suddenly I was sure: he was soon going to return to the world of men and leave me on these deserted shores, because it was actually desirable that I should die all alone. His hand was still holding mine; he squeezed it gently one last time, then went and lay down in a large hollow in the sand.

He pulled a piece of cloth over his face and fell asleep.

I walked about. Our stone tables shone under the summer stars. Our campsite was barely visible except for the white sheet which fluttered in the gentle night breeze. I also lay down on a big bed of sand; I looked at the stars, the beautiful universe I loved, the boundless work of

God, my Creator and my Judge. In the warm, peaceful darkness, disturbed only by the wind on the sheet, my soul trembled joyously at the idea of returning to its God. An indescribable joy took hold of my heart. What did I really have to fear? Had I not been helped many times, protected on the paths that lead to the AWAKENING? And, as a fit ending, this friend had come and held my hand very tightly before leaving me on the threshold of the Most Holy Eternity!

Already up, he was getting ready to leave. We talked quietly in the divine calm of the end of the night. One by one, bright stars were going out in the clear heavens. A sweet smell of lavender and cedar, unique to Athos, mingled with the scents that came from the water, which at this hour was smooth and green.

The after-life frightened him; petty reasons drew him to the mortal side. He was hoping a boat would come past and take him back to the world of men. He could have stayed on the Holy Mountain, happy, without a care. Paradise had not been denied him: it was him who did not want it! Most simple souls soon return to the world, unable to live far from human affairs: family and children call to them. Never adults, they come back quickly to the soft bellies of women, having tasted only for an instant the delights of a life that is free from the shackles of the present century.

A boat had seen his signals. It was not without shame

that he abandoned me on the deserted beach. He left me the provisions: our bread, our cans of oil. He gave me money, like a pious layman who prefers to demonstrate his generosity rather than become a hermit. The boat touched the shore. My annoyance with him suddenly came out: let him go then, without remorse, and leave me to my strange fate!

His eyes full of tears, he took me in his arms. Then he kissed my hands and my face.

"In another life, I will come for ever … " he whispered in my ear.

"Till another life, till another life," I called to him as he went away across the sea.

"Till another death, till another death … " replied the echoes of the Land of the Spirits.

V

THE BURNS

I SPENT THE DAY in the shade of our tree, waiting for what must happen to me. Late in the afternoon I cook my solitary supper. I put some fish to fry in a pan. The oil catches fire! The frying pan, precariously balanced, falls on my right leg, setting fire to my clothes! I give a loud cry and roll on the sand. The flames go out quite quickly. Howling with pain and fear, I wait for the pain to ease. The red-hot oil has burnt me from ankle to waist, the charred material has worked itself into the flesh, which is covered in blisters. Could I get to my feet? For more than an hour I have been stretched out on this shore where nobody ever comes. I am tormented by thirst and my flask is almost empty. I must get to the spring, and at least die near water.

I managed to drag myself to the spring, using a stick to lean on. My right leg can barely move. Kneeling in the mud, drawing water in my hands is long and painful. Gently I pull away the material; an angry wound is weeping, with terrible shooting pains, and the suffering returns suddenly and agonisingly. It is now almost dark: a summer evening, very warm, very blue. The spring is at the bottom of a steep rocky slope. To my left, a track climbs into the hills and heads towards a square tower whose dark mass looms over me, less frightening than brotherly, helpful. Beside the tower there are orange trees and yews, always the sign of a *skete*. This one is probably abandoned. Not a single light. A sort of instinct tells me to get away from the shore, which is already very dark, and to get closer to this orchard that I can see twenty metres above me. My leg is now paralysed; soon I will not be able to walk. My fever is turning to delirium. Now, straight away, I must try and reach this *skete* where I might find help.

Painfully I climb the steep track. With every step the top of my leather boot cuts into the swollen flesh, slices open the blisters, rubs against the burning, sensitive, fiery skin. Taking off my boot would be impossible, so swollen is the ankle, and the idea of having to put a bare, burnt foot on the sharp stones of the track horrifies me. Besides, the *skete* is not much further; I can already see its roof of flat stones.

A wooden gate: I lift its metal hoop at the entrance to an ancient garden. Here there are irrigation streams where clear water flows, orange trees, fragrant lemon trees, olives, yew, their every leaf lit softly by the moon. All is still in the depths of the night, a sort of peaceful savagery. I see whitewashed walls made of dried earth and wooden laths. A staircase leads to the closed door of a sort of farm. No light shines behind the broken panes of several small windows; on the window sills are pieces of fruit, melons and dirty jackets that have almost rotted away. Emerging from the shadows, about to collapse, myself a shadow, I climb the stairs. My fingers grope over the rough wood to find a key, a latch. The door is not locked, I push it open.

I walk into this miserable farmhouse with its walls of daub, and its collapsing floor. The heat of the July evening is stifling. No one. I call out. No voice answers. Moving away from the patch of light thrown by the half-open door, I move on blindly into a narrow corridor and several dark rooms without finding a single piece of furniture, so poor and abandoned does the house seem to be. The corridor leads to a balcony. Right there in the moonlight … on the floor of the half-ruined balcony, an old man is lying on a rotten old mat. Completely naked, terribly thin, he is dying. His breathing is short, weak. He is alone by the sea, which shimmers in the distance between dark reefs. Can he see them? His eyes are empty! Within his reach there is a jug of water, some dry bread, a rosary. He has heard me, and my presence puzzles him. He is so weak he is unable to say a word or move his head; but one fleshless, white arm lifts up and seeks me out. But who am I to him? A stranger, the angel you await at the moment of death? A traveller, for he has certainly noticed that my step is not that of a monk? A presence: a hand that gently takes his; lips that respectfully kiss his old fingers? A quiet voice that asks if he is thirsty? An already divine presence? If someone wanted to go over to the side of the Spirits, and behave like a spirit helping a dying man by bringing him a final consolation, then that was indeed me, that hot summer night in that lonely house on the side of the Holy Mountain, so white beneath the stars.

Has he lost consciousness? He is no longer moving. I have the impression that he has been alone for several days, that he is dying slowly, without suffering, sometimes returning to life: it is the way you end your life on Athos

… alone, naked on a wooden balcony, with water, bread, a rosary by your hand! As for me, I forgot my pain while I was helping the old man. The pain comes back, agonising. I can no longer stand; my useless right leg is on fire and refuses to bear my weight. I look for a bed in this house which smells violently of incense, rancid oil, charcoal, grime and spice … still groping my way, for I have to lean against the wall, as you can see as much in here as you would inside an oven. Not finding a single bed, I lay down on the dusty floor, behind the half-open door through which some air comes.

Did I fall asleep? Later on this hot summer night, I am woken by the door, which someone is trying to open wide, and which bangs against my prone, painful body. They persist, force a way in; one by one two heavy boots, stinking of sweat and leather, step over my head. I hear footsteps in the corridor, the rasp of a match, I see the growing glimmer of a paraffin lamp. A monk, not as old as the one who is dying on the balcony, an overnight bag still over his shoulder, questions me harshly. He seems absolutely furious to find someone lying on his floor after midnight! Then he sees my charred clothes, my burnt leg … He opens a little door, puts the lamp on a shelf, comes back, drags me into a low, narrow room that I had not noticed before, helps me to climb onto a rotten old pallet, shaking, with my boots still on my feet. He brings me water in a tin can, leaves me the lamp, and goes off to busy himself with the other dying man.

The touch of the filthy blankets and the horsehair mattress against my raw leg is unbearable. I turn over onto my left side, drink some water and, shaking, put the tin of water under the bed. I am dying of fever. I am suffocating. My leg is burnt raw; if I put my hand on it a sort of icy shudder runs through me, so sensitive is the skin. The pain echoes the wild beating of my heart; they are dull blows, surges of pain, which die down and then start again. My lungs need air. I am dying. The dry earth walls are oozing heat; the half-darkness, the narrowness of the room are oppressive. The honey-coloured light of the cheap paraffin lamp lights up a rusty nail on which hangs a tiny poor icon whose brownish gold glimmers in the darkened room. I am thirsty. The fever is burning me, my face runs with sweat. You would think I was in a sauna. The pain is terrible but bearable, perhaps because the fever is drugging me. I am burning, I feel I am surrounded by invisible flames. But I have not given up hope; it is only a transmutation; I am passing through fire: I am a soul saved for ever, I know it! I am thirsty; I dare not call out, ask for water; the slightly cold edge of the tin, which I suck at greedily, soothes my parched lips for a moment. So what do I have to atone for, to destroy before the AWAKENING? I see the whole of my destiny over several centuries, not in images but in colours in my mind: the colours of one life, of another. The colours of my eternal soul, gold, orange, blue, the red of live embers! My brain, overheated by fever and fuelled with blood poisoned by the burns, is working at an incredible speed, in a dimension unknown to me, outside time, deep within a universe of colours, of lights and flames. I have not lost consciousness; unexpectedly I remain very lucid: I am at the heart of a swirling inferno whose gigantic flames explode as far as the distant stars. Then, reluctantly, I come back to this pallet in this stifling little room with daub walls where pain is waiting for me. It gnaws at my knee, my thigh, and rises to the groin, before being let loose in my head. With dread I await each surge of pain; my eyes are fixed on the little icon. The gold calms me. A barely visible, filthy, scaly person, burnt by candle flames, stands out on the old gold. Is it Christ, the Virgin or some saint impossible to identify? A shadow, a dark shape offering to help—but no more than an image on the divine gold. My moans, the moans of a burns victim … my sufferings, eased by the sight of a holy shape standing out against a sacred, unchanging gold … this gold that attracts me, and into which I want to dissolve for ever, so I won't suffer any more … I ask myself, am I now crossing a Christian area of the after-life? In this solitary house, could I by chance have stumbled across Purgatory, and the Paradise of the Christians, which is only that of the burnt, the scourged, the martyrs?

The monk—the able-bodied one—has heard my cries, my moans; for I cry out constantly. My head tosses about on the flea-ridden jacket that he has slipped behind my neck; and this poverty, this grimy saint: this is also Christianity! He gives me some water, refills the rusty tin which serves as a cup, helps me drink by lifting my shoulders with simple kindness, as well as that complete indifference so typical of monks who, all their lives, have been waiting for death as a deliverance: their own, and that of others. He examines my burns, which are quite an ugly sight; I would like some oil on my sores … oil, gentle oil, quickly! He says he has none. I am sure he has, but he is keeping it for himself; for the toothless old man who perhaps no longer eats anything but bread soaked in rancid oil. He can do nothing for me. He turns up the wick of the lamp, which immediately lights the icon more clearly. It is better for me to look at God than to ask for oil! God, the sole judge of what I must suffer before going to Him! When the monk has left me, a sort of dialogue begins between the icon and me. No, I am lucid enough to reject this pious illusion! The God of the Christians exists only in the minds of Christians. It is up to me to AWAKEN MYSELF! My sufferings are only a nightmare brought on by the destruction of my being. My sole judge, my sole torturer, is me! Let me go over to the realm of the eternal light and I shall not suffer any more! The compassion for my torments that seems to come from the icon is just an illusion: I love myself, I love others … this gentle side of my nature helps me cross the last thresholds without too much suffering. To call this inclination for charity and forgiveness Jesus Christ is only an illusion; it is to attribute to an idol qualities that belong to me! Suddenly, my soul detaches itself from my burnt body. All suffering disappears; my soul soars above my chest, which has stopped beating; I am filled with inexpressible peace; I climb towards a clear blue sky, boundless, golden, sufficient unto itself, eternal, nameless.

A noise brings me back to myself. Someone is shaking me by the shoulder. It is my host, who is worried about my burns. I have been without any treatment for hours, and having a filthy mattress rubbing against my wounds can't be doing a lot of good, he says, inasmuch as I can hear his voice, which is hardly at all; for I am sinking into a kind of lethargy, complete exhaustion, sleep. The lamp has nearly run out of paraffin, and now throws only a faint trembling light on the dried earth wall.

"Tomorrow Pantocrator," he says.

I understand that he wants to take me to the nearby monastery of Pantocrator, where perhaps they will look after me. It is his duty; what he really means is that he has no desire for me to die in his house. So why did I not die tonight! The hardest part was over! Is it better for me to die later? But after what ordeals! To die older, more lucid, having atoned for everything and learnt everything! If I first tasted the delights of Athos, I am quite certain that I am now going to experience its torments and its sorrows.

He did not even help me on the track that leads to Pantocrator. He set off ahead of me, leaving me to limp along behind. My leg is not as painful this morning, but it is only a respite. Once through the postern gate he as good as abandoned me in the church, where I fell, almost fainting. Meanwhile he was already striding off back home. The monks of Pantocrator have settled me in a fairly clean room. My burn is no better. I am suffering less, but the wound is becoming infected. They have washed it in lukewarm water; I would not go so far as to say that it was boiled. Today, thank God, they bring me news of the most timely arrival … of a great doctor, who is passing through the monastery.

The hoofs of his mule echoed in the courtyard: here is our skilful man.

On Athos you can expect anything; where does he come from? He is dressed more or less like a monk, and no doubt he is a monk, very old, frail, no bigger than a child. A peculiar kind of headgear adorns his birdlike head: lots of pieces of leather roughly sewn together, embellished with badges; a sort of pointed hat in the style of the fifteenth century, with earpieces lifted up at the sides. A cardboard peak held in place by string throws a shadow onto his steel-rimmed glasses and his very pointed nose. Our Hippocrates walks in slowly, not losing an inch of his meagre height, has the shutters half-opened, puts a leather mallet on the table, examines the patient, looks at the urine samples, watched admiringly by seven or eight monks and novices for whom my illness is the big event of the year. Not wanting to miss anything of the show, they have come in procession to my dark room. Stroking his little goatee, our man takes a lancet and probes around mercilessly in the wounds. It makes me moan with pain! He takes no notice. Like a connoisseur, he smells a few drops of pus; the lancet is passed round the room, everyone sniffs the bad smell that comes from it … shakes his head, grimaces, gives me three days to live. Hippocrates, one finger pointing at the sky, calls the novices to be his witness: the eye is yellow, the wounds are festering, the urine cloudy; now we are going to perform a miracle … this poor man here owes the good fortune of finding … a doctor like me … to the intercession of some very great saint.

One finger still pointing at the ceiling, Hippocrates orders that the patient is to be taken to the 'Medicinal Room'. The first outcome of this is that the children are overjoyed. I am dragged from corridor to corridor, all decorated with Apocalypses and Jacob's Ladders, long vaulted passages dimly lit by narrow arrow-slits looking out over the green waves of the Aegean, supremely beautiful under the hot sun of the Greek summer. Dazzled by glimpses of the sea, I let myself be carried, pulled, led almost like a blind man. At the end of a dark corridor we stop at a little scarlet door. Our man takes a bunch of keys from his pocket, opens a hefty padlock, and we enter his consulting room, the most amazing place you could wish to see. They sit me down on a chair. For the novices … to enter the Medicinal Room … is a rare event; for our skilled practitioner goes from monastery to monastery at the gentle pace of his mule; a vast tour of duty which seldom brings him to Pantocrator. He alone has the key to the room of marvels, which is always locked in his absence. Some of the novices, who are among the youngest, appear never to have even seen it, and are wide-eyed. A stuffed crocodile, the worse for wear, losing its horsehair stuffing, hangs from the ceiling by an intricate system of ribbons. A window looking onto the sea throws sunlight onto a writing case, a desk, some cats' skulls, preserved vipers, flasks of wine of mandrake, a collection of elixirs of youth, lots of shelves full of faience and earthenware pots, their old labels covered with an elegant Byzantine writing fading with the years. An icon gives a pious note to this cubby-hole of extravagances. Our man is at home here, acts important, pulls down my trousers and feels my knee, consults texts ten times older than he is; while on my chair, half-naked, I await the help of his art.

It is as if I have been forgotten. It is the crocodile that attracts the novices' attention. They exclaim over the length of its tail, its teeth frighten them. Is it really dead? Some of them are sure it opened one eye, that it moved the tip of its tail! They are asked to be quiet, and threatened with a beating; they fall silent, for … Hippocrates has found the balm I need! With solemn movements, all ecclesiastical self-importance and dignity, rolling up his sleeves, our great doctor chooses … a jar: this one; not another! The lid is undone, not without difficulty … for the said jar … seems to have been firmly closed … since the fourth crusade! Our doctor shows round an exquisite balm, sweetly scented, very old, venerable. He gets me to smell it, declares it three times blessed, infallible. To hear him talk, my cure is assured: this jar contains all the secrets of the apothecary's art.

"Plus … " he adds, "and this is not the least of it … a tear of Saint John Chrysostom!"

With the flat of his hand he rubs a smooth, honey-coloured, sweet-smelling cream on my burns. It soaks deep into the swollen flesh. The novices miss nothing of the process, suddenly all pious, tipsy with the delightful smell that comes from the pot and fills the room. They put my trousers back on. I ask this skilful man if I owe him a few drachmas. He is about to answer … that he practises in a spirit of Christian charity … when suddenly I pass out! They rush around, they lay me on the floor; they send for a strong gardener who carries me to my room like a bundle of logs.

My burns are healing. This balm, as old as the world, has secret properties; as does perhaps my age, for despite my present appearance I know I am very old. Is this the first time I have been given shelter, sick and wounded, in a monastery on Athos? I am sure not! I often think I see my distant past more clearly than this life. From my bed I sometimes hear the hammer-blows calling the monks to church, and the sound of the cold surf pounding the foot of the walls some two hundred metres beneath my room. What is to become of me? I am not a monk. I have no place in any monastery. I am not even a Christian; I am a traveller who wants to journey to the AWAKENING.

Monks! The advancement of your soul is the last thing these poor dolts think of! Are you a mason, a locksmith, a roofer? You are their man immediately! It matters little to them that your devotions are pure hypocrisy … if you can repair a roof! For these people, who, like all idiots, have absolutely nothing to do, will not let up for a minute, so completely occupied are they with this, then that, whatever comes into their head. Some idiot wants a wall for his garden; another wants his bedroom ceiling painted blue; this one says his lock squeaks. Woe betide the poor traveller who can't use a trowel. A waster like that can clear off to the woods! In the monasteries you are judged only by your workmanlike abilities. They have little saintliness; they only have fads … This one wants a water-clock: the monk thinks about it, loses sleep over it, dreams about it, looks for a skilful workman, asks advice from the innkeeper, his best friends, his dear ones. Years go by. Apart from beautiful boys, the idiot is still toying with his beloved plan for a hydraulic clock.

The innkeeper … has heard … that a certain cobbler … knows a bit about clocks. The man is sought out, for the monk insists on having his clock. Not with a pendulum, not with a weight, not with music, not with pedals. A water-clock! The innkeeper is guarded; the cobbler used to repair clocks … water-clocks; but he can't say for sure. The monk becomes impatient; the man is impossible to find; Athos is vast! How do you find a retired cobbler? The monk gets angry. But then he regains hope: one of his dear little favourites actually knew a brother or a cousin of the cobbler; a very skilful man, claims the adolescent, lowering his eyes so demurely. The monk listens. He can no longer contain his delight. This brother, or this cousin, is bound to have inherited a few scraps of knowledge about water-clocks from his relative the cobbler … So it is decided to set off after this cousin, who is currently a roofer … somewhere near Iviron. Monk and darlings wait all summer for a mule-train to pass by. Here are the animals; they climb into the saddle, delighted to be going on a trip. One fine morning they spot the said cousin: yes, it is him, down by the sea, trowel in hand, up an old roof repairing the gutters. They shout to him. Cautiously the rogue comes down his ladder. He knows nothing about clocks, but sees there are a few drachmas to be had. To hear him talk you would think he invented the hydraulic mechanism. He wants a thousand drachmas! But that's daylight robbery! The monk refuses outright, but gives in at six hundred. This will be for next year … when the monk … gets … a small sum which comes to him each year from a vineyard … that he let out … to one of his colleagues … when it was necessary … to make sensible provision for a favourite who was getting older. Finally he sets to work on the clock. An extremely antique clock, lifeless since the war of 1914, is taken to bits, then put back together again quite differently. A system of pipes … held on by string, brings water from a barrel … into a zinc basin … in which a wooden ball floats. As this slowly sinks … because of … a little hole in the bottom of the basin, it sets gears in motion. It works when it wants to. It is hideous, it looks like nothing on earth! Word gets round that such and such a monastery owns a fine water-clock, and that people come from far away to gaze at it. Well: multiply the STORY OF THE WATER-CLOCK ad infinitum. Imagine that each monk has his own pet craze. In other words, since I am not a builder and know nothing about hydraulic mechanisms, these decent, harmless people have no need of me; just as I am not keen on their pretty mediocre company. The holy caves! To return to the Sacred Forest, to be a hermit! I must end my days alone. The sooner the better.

I can already drag myself as far as the church. Standing in one of the stalls, I lean against an arm-rest to ease the pain a little. The sight of the gold calms my fever. The singing, the scent of the incense in the middle of the afternoon, help my soul free itself from the weight of its past. The happy time of my carefree existence is over. I am now no more than a wounded man, a burns victim. I am called to the marble doorway, a heavy hanging is pulled aside: in the blazing sunshine, mule-drivers are having a discussion with the monks. A mule-train has just arrived; it is a chance for me to go to Kariés, to get closer to the region of the holy caves; it is a chance for them to get rid of a patient whose presence will eventually be a nuisance. They ask me to leave: I am not able to get on a mule, especially as they are very big, and seem bad-tempered and likely to kick. Never mind, they will haul up me into the saddle. The price? Three hundred drachmas to take me to Kariés. I suggest two hundred. We come to an agreement: okay, but there will not be a 'man' to guide me. They will put me on a mule and, since the honest beast knows the tracks perfectly, she will take me of her own accord to Kariés where she has her stable. As the saying goes, don't spare the horses! Well, why not? Once the decision is made, the monks drift away. Shaking their black robes, they head back to their dark retreats. The mule-drivers go for a *raki* in a cool kitchen, out of the terrible sun. The courtyard is empty. An old servant helps me get up on an animal, leads it by the bridle to the gate of the monastery, gives me the reins, strokes the mule, whispers a few words in its ear, and taps it on the backside, pushing it outside.

Ducking my head, I go under a cold, sad archway. Without a goodbye, like a pauper, I leave Pantocrator with a subdued sound of hoofs on the flagstones.

Here is the motionless sea. Here are slopes cobbled with round pebbles, dropping steeply to walled kitchen gardens where young peas climb vigorously up long sticks. My mount, its head down, stumbles with every step, threatening to throw me. I seat myself more securely on the wooden saddle and hang on to the girth. Once over a bridge, the mule straightway climbs into the countryside at a good pace, and does actually seem to know the way back to its stable.

I was expecting the worst: a fall, appalling pain. But by some magic all goes well. The stirrup supports my injured leg. The mid-afternoon heat would be unbearable if I was on foot and had to climb the steep slopes, covered with bushes and wild olive trees which, to the sound of the cicadas, stand up straight in sight of the shimmering sea. Thank God my mule carries me cheerfully! I turn round in the saddle. The battlemented tower of Pantocrator is now no more than a light patch against the distant water. Crippled by my burns, I was like a prisoner in that ancient monastery. But here I am, travelling again, off to become a hermit! Could I ask for anything more cheerful, more likely to appeal to me, a luckier twist of fate? I have money in my saddlebags: after many wanderings, all of them symbolic, I am heading for Wisdom. I am on the way to the AWAKENING.

VI

THE ALCHEMICAL RETREAT

DID I LIVE on Athos for many years, or just a few months? I can still remember an incredibly vast time, what seems like an entire life; a time at once immense and very short, whose uncertain duration remains a puzzle to me.

No one was waiting for me in the Sacred Forest … or rather, destiny was waiting for me, and soon proved to be utterly tragic. I found neither Joshua nor the monk. They had disappeared! The door of their *skete* was closed. I call in vain. I break open the door. Everything in their poor house smells of abandonment. They have gone for good! No one lives in these woods any more. That is because wandering is a compulsion on Athos: you come, you go; you are invited somewhere, you hide your keys under the brambles; you come back in six months, you don't come back at all … At the time I was delighted by this departure, which satisfied my taste for pillage. But I did not realise that when my solitude became agonising I would soon be disillusioned. A saucepan and a lamp would do nicely; I carried them off to my cave. Very quickly I felt at home; I no longer left the banks of the stream. The song of the cicadas and the screech of the night birds kept me company, but in the end they would frighten me.

One cave proved to be habitable, and even had a big deep fireplace. As soon as night fell I lit a fire in it, cooking myself scanty meals, ever more modest out of economy and from disgust with food. Solitude shrunk my stomach. I would forget to eat for two or three days, without suffering too much from this dangerous abstinence. I even found it gave me a sensation of slight, and by no means unpleasant intoxication, which however gave way to an appalling sadness as evening came. If the truth be known, I was more an alchemist than tempted by some form of saintliness; I was waiting for 'something', a transformation of my deepest being. This solitude and fasting was heading towards suicide; I would have been aware of this fact if I had not been constantly occupied. But I had got it into my head to write the story of my adventures on the Holy Mountain. I wrote on the rocks, beside the water, and then in bed by the glow of my paraffin lamp, later and later into the night, putting into my account a joy of living that was already deserting me. I enjoyed seeing my youth again, my carefree wanderings, my happy loves, while at the same time the years were already weighing heavily on me. For I was getting older from day to day, with a speed that was out of proportion with the few months that had passed since I came to live in the Sacred Forest. Autumn was nearly over. I had lived here for three months, no more: and I had aged a hundred years! As far as I could make out in a little mirror … growing a beard had hidden the face of a man who was already getting old. But in the depths of my being, an insurmountable tiredness made me feel that the adolescent I had been for a very long time was becoming an old man.

No longer surprised by the magic of the Land of the Spirits, I accepted my new state with a sort of curiosity.

I put down the speed of this transformation down to the special properties of time on this side of life, which seemed capable of passing very quickly, then very slowly, of breaking up, of rejecting life, only to reappear according to mysterious laws that I could still not grasp.

My health is no longer what it was. Since the autumn I have had a suffocating sensation in my chest which comes on whenever I make the least effort; so much so that I am unable to go and cut wood in the forest because of this peculiar pain which racks me whenever I use the axe or bend down to pick up firewood. Instead I make do with taking what I need to keep the fire going from an old supply of beams and logs. I light it at dawn and poke it until evening, sitting on my cooking pot, which is my only seat since I burnt my chair. I write all day long, crouched over a plank laid across my knees, dipping my pen in an inkwell I have set up on a firedog, simmering insipid broth in my poor saucepans, and watching with horror as my small supply of tea and sugar dwindles.

When the sky is clear I go into the forest, not venturing too far for fear that when I get back the fire will have gone out; not so much because I am short of matches, but because the fire is the only companion I have left in my appalling loneliness. The winter promises to be harsh; an old overcoat and my Luftwaffe boots keep me fairly warm. I return before nightfall, eager to see my fire again, my cooking pot, my saucepans, eager to get back to my bed where I feel safe, going to bed early, fully dressed, writing until about three o'clock in the morning, delighted to have my notebooks, my ink-well, my pen-holder and my lamp around me. Then, forgetting my distress, I quickly write down the story of my wanderings in the time of my youth. A time that seems very far off. Curiously, I have no memory of the middle of my life; I passed suddenly from youth to old age, jumping over maturity. Anyone would think the beginning and the end of a destiny were the only parts that mattered to me. For I love only the dawn and the evening. My true self is that of a child, of an old man. "The old man and the child": that phrase sometimes sings in my head, without conjuring up anything in particular; but it belongs to me in some way, it comes to me from another life. Which one? I have no idea. The Voyage of the Dead, The Sorcerer's Apprentice, 'that' concerns me too, without my knowing why. I am now no more than a spirit, which having renounced the pleasures that were awaiting it in the after-life, is filled with dread as it feels the increasing weight of loneliness and sorrow, which it deserved to feel, made worse by this chest pain which takes away the joy of living and only eases in bed. My bed: a platform cut high up in the rock, at the very back of my cave. Where I cannot climb except by standing on a stone. It is less a bed than an encampment where I have my blankets, my short metal sword, my lamp and my bowl of tea. What time is it? Past midnight … someone is walking in the stream; dragging their feet very noticeably.

The cliffs are haunted, I know that. Presences emerge from the woods, approach my entrance. One night, by the glow of my dying embers, I saw Joshua sitting on the corner of the hearth. More often they are souls from nature, dead animals, trees that want to be reborn, ancient rocks that dream or monks who used to live in this cave. Being a great medium, I attract them. I am not afraid of the ghosts, but of my own destiny, which in the after-life is called the consequences of past actions. I put down my pen on the blanket, covered with blotches of ink: here ends the story of my first wanderings on the Holy Mountain; more than twenty notebooks. A great dream is completed. Here I am, coming back to my present state. I blow out the lamp. The last flames of the fire light up my cave. The lack of food makes me extremely weak, without any defence against the final echoes of my basest instincts. The feminine part of my nature comes back to the surface and takes the place of a wife. I carved a piece of wood in the shape of a penis, I sodomized myself; then, furious with this stupidity, I threw the foul-smelling bit of wood into the ashes, wondering nonetheless whether such perversity is not part of some arcane art of AWAKENING, so old that it is now regarded as appalling. If this were true, my nature would be older than history; it would date back to the first nights, the first fires, when men lived in caves.

A quiet light enters my stone room. It has snowed during the night. Heavy flakes fell silently while I was writing. I light a fire. The bright red flames at the back of my fireplace make a strange contrast with the white of the snow, which, under a very blue sky, covers the frozen banks of the stream. I pull the cooking pot up to the entrance and sit down with my back against the damp rock. So why did I not die at the height of my youth, carefree and happy? What must I atone for? No doubt I have to drain the consequences of my past acts right down to the dregs. Before the AWAKENING I must finish freeing myself from the weight of my many lives. A powerful transformation is at work within me, perhaps without my knowing. Am I at the end of my sufferings? There is justice in the after-life: I have never liked humans; as a result I am dying alone, far from men, without the help of men.

The solitary life is an alchemical experience, a transmutation of the being that is not without danger. You must patiently burn away all impurity before hoping to see in yourself the Clear Primordial Light. Can I help my soul to free itself from the last ties that bind it? Since everything is only calls, echoes, resonance, is it possible to do it by incantation, by magic?

I decided to make myself a musical instrument. Since I was almost destitute it would have to be rather primitive. Using an old metal drum as an echo chamber, I nailed on a heavy board with a round hole in it. Wooden pegs enabled me to tension some strong supple nylon threads I found in a drawer in the *skete*, which were probably used for fishing. A small movable board, which altered the depth of pitch, completed my creation. I carried it to a narrow crevice halfway up the cliffs. It was hardly a cave, as I could not stand upright in it, but it had one advantage: from there the view stretched right over the forests to the bright marble of Athos.

The rough surface of the rock bruised my shoulders and my back terribly. I hugged my warm woollen coat tightly round me, and, sitting up straight, my heavy boots pulled under my thighs, I took up the lotus position, having no wish to prostrate myself before gods who, even if they exist, are themselves only ancient dreamers. I made peace with myself, I breathed slowly. Freezing cold air, which smelt of dead leaves and humus, went deep down into my lungs. I held my breath; the damp and the bitter cold swept through me. Feeling sorry for myself would have served no purpose at the point I had reached in my destiny. I had distanced myself from humans to become an adult at last, alone in the face of the Awakening, unlamenting in the rocky hole where I had hidden myself, a hundred metres above a fast-flowing stream.

My musical instrument, lying across my thighs, attracted me. This object, made with my own hands, was a part of me, filled with my desires, my tendencies. I wanted to hear the sound it made. I closed my eyes; I touched a string: it vibrated intensely in the cramped cave, which made the resonance even stronger. Another string: this was a new aptitude of my spirit, which sang in the absolute silence.

From string to string I explored the different powers of my soul. Was my true self, like space and time, nothing but resonance and sounds, taken up by many different echoes? I was getting closer to the Awakening, if only through the distinct feeling of time exploding; more precisely, I was beginning to see its real nature: it does not flow like a river; it breaks up, forever changing, forever returning to non-existence, only to reappear—not further forward, but elsewhere.

Faced with intermittent time, I had to see myself, from age to age, from a viewpoint that was also constantly being broken apart, shattered. I had to acknowledge not so much that the self is only an illusion, but rather that it can reveal itself at the same moment in different places and times, that it is capable of ceasing to be, so that it can be reborn. I did not lack courage: so why not try and live in that dimension? Why not accept real time, real space, constantly changing?

The Byzantine painters had also had a sense of the real. Through love of gold I had brought an icon into this rocky fissure. I opened my eyes: the Nazarene was enthroned in glory, surrounded by a pattern of multicoloured rectangles and circles strangely interpenetrating. He stood in the centre of a space, book in hand. At first sight it seemed utterly absurd! Yet this 'naive' painting was not so far from reality. To understand the real, even though it is contrary to all apparent logic; to know that in this cave I was—also—elsewhere, without ceasing to be myself, without ceasing to be here; so why reject this adventure of the spirit, I thought, looking at a sky that was dark, icy-blue, and which, as evening came, turned an almost-black violet above the pure marble slopes of the Holy Mountain.

Suddenly I felt dizzy, and almost passed out. Not only was I shivering with anguish and cold, but moving to a higher level of consciousness also meant that I could no longer ignore the problematic nature of my existence, whose constant transformations, in different times, had driven away for ever all notion of identity. Several times during my adventures on Athos, I had got a glimpse of this lack of true identity, and noticed frequent disappearances of time. This evening the certainty of being only a soul, an aspect of the divine cast endlessly into an unbelievably vast space, and into several constantly disconnected times, made me frightened.

I thought I was destroyed. Then I came to, back to at least one of my possible lives. But who was I? I had acquired a taste for indescribable freedom! Perhaps very unhappy, I would not have wanted to return to a half-sleep: to be only a man, shut away in one time, in a single life, and in a single condition. I remembered having lived a hundred times, always the same yet each one different, an alchemist in Byzantium, a monk in Russia, on Athos, in Asia! To me, my true self was only an archetype, linked to many different adventures, to continual echoes. What the Indians call 'karma'. I watched it with detachment, even though it interested me enormously … its joys, like its sorrows, seemed only to be those of a friend I had always known. The Awakening; no doubt I had been prepared for it for a long time; my spirit grew calmer and got used to its new life.

The moon rose above the forests in a winter sky. I gathered together a few stones and some dry wood at the entrance to my little cave. I lit a fire, made some tea, still sitting on the ground, legs folded under me, kindling the flames with slow, measured, very Asiatic movements. I came from Asia—or somewhere else! For a moment I was almost sure I came from the future, from a world and a civilization that knew the real nature of space and time. Then this intuition was wiped away; my water was boiling, I threw in a pinch of tea; I picked up the saucepan, put it down it beside me, still breathing slowly, then holding my breath.

My flames dead, the glow of a red ember burnt through the darkness. Thousands of stars, and the perfect disc of the moon were now shining in a black sky. Again I was seized with fear. The change to a higher state of consciousness had to be won from an appalling panic. I had the impression of falling into the void! Mustering all my will-power I returned to my present state, to this rocky hole. I stirred up the embers, drank my tea. This evening it was as if I had reached a point of breaking away. From now on I could believe that my nature, my tendencies, my virtues and vices would survive for ever in all possible times. Trembling with fear, I accepted my new condition. In all my lives I had loved the sky, but in an enchanted, adolescent way. This evening I watched the stars with a gaze that was unknown to me: my soul, awakened to its true dimensions and an adult at last, was sharing in the secret movements of the perfect constellations. Looking at the sky, I was a new being, absent from itself—FOR EVER PRESENT in the universe! This equation now seemed very normal, self-evident; I would not have wanted to give up this new vision, or go back to a primitive opinion of man, space and time. Yet it took a great effort of will not to flee the terrifying state that mine had become, beyond all personal identity. But I was not 'the others'; I was myself at last, a mentally adult man who is discovering his real dimension in the universe, and who for the first time gives his soul to the time of the stars.

I was slowly getting used to this new state. The unpredictable resurgence of primeval terrors seemed to be fading, giving way to a divine peace.

The moon spread a peaceful, sacred glow over the rocks, leaving me and my rocky fissure in deep shadow. Again I picked up the musical instrument that was resting on my knees; I leant the heavy board of this poor harp on one shoulder. It was cold enough to split rocks. With a frozen finger I plucked a string: it reverberated, then fell silent. Using vibrations, could I dispel the chaos of dreams, awaken the pure sound and, through it, conquer my old fears? I improvised a glass-like music in the presence of eternity. Crystal clear, my strings sang in the brilliant night, studded with stars and constellations. After so much pride, after so much strange idleness, yet full of potential, disinterested in myself, I gave myself up to this shining space. With all my new soul I shared in the glory of the stars. A string vibrated, and divided time into delightful moments; another one called me to the Awakening. Then, as the sounds moved on, they all found pure chords. The slow vibrating of the strings became frenzied; the sweet strings beneath my fingers, the sounds they made, it was me: broken, shattered, despairing, overjoyed.

I was suffering less from cold and loneliness. At least I could admit that I was alone, at such a time in my life! I carried on playing; using the resonance, I freed myself from my ancient fears. The music purified, destroyed, rebuilt my soul. The basic tendencies of my nature ... already no longer belonged to me. I saw them outside myself, outside time, available; they were becoming unfamiliar to me. Another state of mind was taking their place, harder, more lucid, totally committed to the starry sky. I paused; my anguish did not cloud my joy; the discovery of real time, real space, and the beauty of this freezing night delighted me. It was what I had always wanted.

I picked up my musical instrument again, this time not wanting to hear anything except the pure sound of the strings. I was attaining wisdom, but in a wild state! When I stopped to think about it, my presence in the region of the caves coincided with the total decline of the Holy Mountain. The unforeseen successor to the pious anchorites: in the land of the worshippers of Christ and the Virgin, I was not a Christian. No doubt I was an artist. In a trance, bursts of light flashed across my mind; I was certain of it: a great power for dreaming and contemplation was going to appear in mankind. For a second I was again certain that I came from the future, then the thought was wiped away. But the conviction remained that I was an enemy of Christianity, this religion of simple folk, destined to quickly die out. The NEW

BEING came from the depths of the human psyche, and from all points of time and space—the real, adult man, the man of the future, the worshipper of the heavens who was being born in me, and who took over from the ancient solitaries who had been in love with Jesus in these caverns. So why should he not be an ARTIST, in a world that has no other goal than to become aware of its own splendour!

A strange artist, in fact, playing the harp in an icy fissure. A primitive forerunner of the man to be born, I was dying of cold and anguish, happy, singing under the stars. For I was singing. An incantation came from my lips. An artist on the brink of the pure Awakening, on a winter night under a polar sky, in a lost gorge of the divine universe. Time and space broken, my joy, my surprise and my happy delirium were no more than music, words, the whisper of the soul, song, the sound of strings! With my metal can gripped firmly between my feet, and the wooden keys resting on my forehead, so much sound was echoing in my head, almost the sound of God, almost the primordial sound. My fingers ran over the strings from low to high; all I had to do was move the bridge, a simple little board, and to change the register and the key, to alter everything, to call everything into question, as you pass from one life to another. With the bridge slightly moved, music from India became a melody of old Europe, then Africa, then Asia once more. I was playing humanity's past, my own. More often, very pure, crystalline sounds that resembled no known music, and which came from the future, rose up to the stars.

It must have been very late. For a long time I had been able to withstand the cold by means of energy, and also courage. I had to leave this rocky fissure and head for my bed. I set off along a path round the cliff, on the edge of emptiness. Bright moonlight lit up the rocks that jutted out above my head, but the narrow track that I hesitated to take without a light was left in total darkness.

Some of my embers were still burning. I gathered them up in a metal saucepan and blew gently on it; a pretty flame dispelled the darkness. I ventured back out onto the cliff path, holding up the saucepan at arm's length, with a faint, uncertain, dancing glimmer guiding my steps. I went down the side of the cliff towards my cave, the icon under my coat. Half-burnt incense must have been mixed in with the glowing coals, for a grey, sweetly-scented smoke followed my slow progress. You would have thought I was burning incense to the stars, alone, by a river late at night.

I stopped to get my breath back. Standing, I leant against the damp rock, with the saucepan at my feet. The brands were going out, but a delicate, delightful fragrance still drifted through the air.

It was one of the most beautiful winter nights I have seen. The harshness of the cold made the starry sky like a pure equation of crystal and fire. Beyond the dark cliffs the Milky Way sparkled with amazing clarity. Countless constellations existed in all possible times: stars born thousands of years ago were going to appear in several black holes in space; a dead star was still glowing, still alive in front of my eyes; young, virgin constellations were gently pulsing; unforeseeable nebulae, spread through the universe as cosmic dust, belonged only to the future. The moon's divine mirror fascinated and attracted me; tonight, in the clear air, you would have thought it was a block of ice, closer to the earth than usual.

I could not take my eyes off the Holy Eternity, which is God, of the COSMOS—LIVING BEING. Creation is not yet finished. It wants to continue, and to find itself in the consciousness of a superior human type. In a sense, I thought, my being here in this lost gorge, my solitude and my anguish, call—for the time being—not so much for the appearance of a new psyche, but rather prove the temporary defeat of a human type with a superior gift for contemplation, a divine race older than history, forced to flee, to take refuge in holes in the rock. I am alone in this region of caves, without wife or child: but would I want to have a son, if it is not from You, O radiant Eternity? For I love You, O Eternity.

Beautiful flames warmed me up quite quickly. I burnt almost the last of my logs. Then, using my stool, I climbed onto the platform where my blankets were. Right at the back of the cave, it was an old hayloft, so crudely cut out of the rock with great chisel-blows that it retained a primordial appearance, and seemed as old as the world. I felt safe here. Within easy reach I could set out my pen-holder, my lamp and my supply of sugar kept dry in a metal tin, and rest my ink-well in a hole that might have been there expressly for the purpose. Up here, in this big stone bed, I had brought my saucepan full of boiling tea. Now, in the middle of the night, I felt no desire at all for sleep. When I was young I slept like a log. With the coming of old age, it was with regret that I felt my eyelids grow heavy. I slept little, constantly staying up all night, thanks to the tea I was always drinking, and because I was reaching a divine state.

Refusing to sleep increased my mental faculties tenfold. I saw the universe in all its glory, and my true situation in relation to the furthest stars. Like it, I was eternal! To have lived for ever, from life to life—and to know it—that is the true dimension of the awakened man, of the real man whose thousand-year duration goes back to the time of the stars. Which is not that of humans! From a certain level of consciousness onwards, the future is not necessarily further forward, but elsewhere; life and death, what is experienced and what is imagined, past and present, are no longer seen as contradictory.

From this perspective, pen-holder in hand, I reread the account of my adventures on the Holy Mountain. What connected the happy adolescent who travelled all over Athos to the old man I had become? It was simply the projection of one single being onto different times. Should I even believe in such a thing as spiritual progress? My present haunted, holy delirium was worth no more or less than the wanderings and debauchery of that inquisitive boy—me!

In his way, Joshua had been my servant and my son, and an adolescent part of my eternal soul, met by chance: someone I loved in a former life, found, then lost again; but who could reappear. Had I been Eric Strauss, whose clothes I had worn for a while before selling them to an innkeeper, who had been eager to give them to one of his mule-driver friends? In another life had I really been that young German soldier, a philosophy graduate, on a special mission to Mount Athos at a time when other Germans were sent to Nepal or Tibet by the government of the Third Reich? Yes and no; I had not been Strauss—but only just! Like him I rejected Christianity, and wanted to renounce a rationalistic view of the world for a magical thought—I had read his notebooks. If I had been born in Munich twenty years earlier, in all probability I would have been that German. I had been Strauss for a few hours! Unforeseeably, this Aryan side of my nature came up against the Slavic, nomadic mentality of a man who was a monk in Russia. Further back, or at the same time, I had known Asia. Was the Athos I loved, and spoke about in this story, the same one you can see on maps? Or was it actually another one, very similar, close in minute details, but parallel, and located in the after-life?

I had known Byzantium and Europe. I was in this cave, and elsewhere. If I wanted to know who I was, I was ending up in an incredible cosmic dimension, pushing back the limits of experience, of the possible, further and further to infinity. Writing by the faint glow of the lamp, I had told my story up as far as this night of vigil. Continuing on, I wrote the next part: what was going to happen to me now, my final wanderings. Quickly I brought my account to its end; I finished my journey on the Holy Mountain! All that remained for me to do now was to live out what I had foreseen.

It was the very end of the night, the delicious moment when, in an incredible silence, everything seems to be sleeping in the hands of the pure and calm Eternity which men call God. In this lost gorge, I was sure of it; mysterious curves, elsewhere and in a different time, brought everything back to Him.

I took another look at my icon. Christ was enthroned, completely motionless, a book in his hand, at the centre of a pattern of red rectangles and black circles, interpenetrating at several points.

Seen naively it was not reality, but the symbol of an unfathomable mystery: God, Primordial Light, uncreated, alone exists at the heart of a space that is subject to strange distortions, often broken up, meeting itself in all possible dimensions; a space spread across infinity—while returning to its point of departure which it has never left. I was not a Christian, but the design of the icon was still valid. Although unbelievable at first, it was true. In the silence of the night I felt that an enormous part of the universe was slowly coming back towards God, while another was moving away.

I put my icon in a cleft in the rock. The lamp, whose wick was getting black, gently lit up the unchanging gold, to me the very image of the Divine Light that attracted me. I sat in the lotus position, my back against the stone, with blankets over my shoulders and thighs, protecting me from the cold. I created silence and peace within myself. I heard the soft murmuring of the stream. In this cave I was alone, close to my end. But the adult man is always alone. If time and space are nothing but resonance and sounds, I thought, would silence not be the secret path by which everything returns to uncreated life?

In the morning I sit down on my cooking pot, not lighting a fire, as my supply of wood is running out. Besides, the fall of snow has taken the edge off the bitter cold of the last few days. It gives off a cheerful, even light. The sky is clear, very blue. Everything is quiet, the colours very intense: the forest, the stream, the thickets in front of the red rocks.

A divine peace overcomes me, going right to the depths of my being, purified by music and fasting, and to my soul, beaten down by pain, detached from selfish interests, empty. Any impure thought would hinder me, but none comes to mind; my past seems to have been banished, the moment itself is enough to make me happy. A ray of sunlight touches my icon, placed in the entrance of the cave.

Sitting on my cooking pot, from the darkness of my hearth, I look at this little piece of wood, painted with divine gold—tarnished by the centuries—washed by the delicate morning light. Alchemical work? In me, everything is calm and silence in order to be nothing but a gaze … the soul becomes what it gazes at. We must die to Time so we can be reborn as Light. Gold attracts me; it is the final idol before seeing God. Idle shadow of the heavens overflowing with brightness! Pious imagery matters little to me. Absent, present … am I alive, am I dead? My hope reaches perfection. O memory of heaven seen again! At the sight of gold my patience is infinite: getting up, leaving my cooking pot, I move the icon along the rock so that the sun can touch it again when it shifts because of the earth's rotation. Then I go back to my cast-iron seat; hours pass; I wait for 'something'. Today, several favourable circumstances seem to come together; the purity of my soul, the evenness of the daylight polarized by the snow.

I close my eyes. What is this weakness that is taking hold of me? I am moving on somewhere else. Do not think, my soul; stay peaceful. Hold your breath, remember your inexistence. THAT which has no NAME shines beneath your closed eyelids, grows as big as the universe, knows nothing about you and has known you for all Eternity. It is the Clear Primordial Light that refuses to be born! Do not be afraid, do not lose consciousness. Look at the Pure Reality: recognise it; it is You. Universal, happy, shining. Stay within It, listen: the pure work of an eternal cause, it sings at the heart of an incredible silence. Living gold, brighter than a thousand suns, it dances without moving: such aimless work, sufficient to fill it with joy!

When I came to I could not have said if I had seen the Clear Primordial Light for a century or for the blink of an eye. In the blue sky a crow was soaring … at the very same moment that I suddenly passed on to absolute existence … it occupied the same point in space: with a flap of its wings, it swooped down onto the top of a tree.

Under its weight some powdery snow fell from the upper branches. It cawed, and then silence fell again. I stood up, walked around a little in the entrance to the cave. There was still an inexpressible joy, a sweetness, a bedazzlement in me, caused by the discovery of an unknown force field of incredible strength. It permeated my whole being. Then the spell disappeared, and only my deepest memory retained intact, the image of the Clear Primordial Light.

I lit a fire. From somewhere around my heart, a worrying pain ran through my left shoulder and down as far as my wrist. In another life, had I been the old alchemist I had become: sick and extremely poor? Or was it simply a mask that for a time covered my true, eternally adolescent face?

Day was breaking over the wild gorge. Mist covered the stream. Above the rocks an extraordinary sky—blue, gold, very pure—meant that beyond the forest the sun was already shining. I went down to the water. Standing on the stones, I stared for a long time at the clear, peaceful, divinely beautiful sky, full of light, which contrasted with the dark cliffs. This golden, crystalline sky, where the pale moon gleamed softly beyond the tall cedars, as though left behind by the night, seemed to be the most exquisite expression of the Clear Primordial Light that I had seen the night before in the depths of my pure consciousness. Of course, it was not It; it was Its loveliest reflection. On this occasion, yet again, I was not a Christian. The strange wisdom that was rising up in me came straight from Asia. Too old, too ancient to believe in Jesus Christ, if I had to 'see' an incarnation of God in the world … then, between the wonderful radiance of the sun rising above the milky mist covering the frozen water of a stream … and the sad figure of a carpenter from Nazareth … I did not hesitate for a moment.

The pain in my chest is getting so much worse that I will have to go into one of the monasteries. It is urgent. I must go straight away, down along the shallow bed of the stream to Koutloumousiou, where I shall be safe and looked after; for I am going to collapse from starvation, from weakness. I gather up my manuscripts, tie them neatly in a bundle and attach it to the leather belt round the waist of my coarse woollen overcoat.

Going along the river I head for Koutloumousiou, dreaming of a square meal. In this region of holy caves I saw the Clear Primordial Light, but at the cost of what terrible solitude! I shall go further towards wisdom, but cautiously, perhaps withdrawing into some monastery or other. In fact, after a long, entirely alchemical retreat into the Sacred Forest, the thought of travelling the paths of Athos one last time in search of new adventures will not be upsetting to my fundamentally Slavic, nomadic, probably Russian nature. I take my manuscripts with me: *The Art of the Sacred Book* can accommodate a wandering genius! Brilliant or not, I am hungry.

VII

THE FINAL PAGES

I MADE ONLY A SHORT STOP at Koutloumoussi, then quickly headed for Kariés, where I knew how to find an excellent inn. My sufferings were not over; I was expecting new ordeals, but I was sure there would be a respite from my misfortunes. It was as if kindly presences were discreetly accompanying me.

Happily I climbed the hundred steps that led to the first narrow streets of Most Holy Kariés. The snow crunched under my boots, the sky was blue over the forests of Athos; above the white roofs, a biting wind was blowing scented smoke around. Everyone kicked their boots, heavy with snow, against the doorsteps of the shops, beat their clothes and roared with laughter. The arrival of the snow was the main topic of conversation; more than one solitary gardener seemed to have come to Kariés for the sole pleasure of telling everyone that he had not seen so much snow since the beginning of the century. As for me, in a very good mood, I wandered along the alley-ways and the passages that lead to the stables, which had a good smell of hay, leather and dung, whose intoxicating scent fuelled my desire to take to the roads once again. If before I had laughed at the rustic appearance of the pious anchorites, today I had to admit that I was beginning to look rather like them. My untrimmed beard made me seem very old; my holed boots were no better than theirs; and I must cut a fine figure with my poor overcoat, dragged in at the waist by a leather belt from which hung an enormous bundle of manuscripts. And, like all solitary people, I had an incredible desire to talk. I went into the little shops, with their frost-covered floors, on the pretext of asking the time, coming out immediately, only to walk in somewhere else with no particular reason. With this one difference: they were among friends, fell into each other's arms, greeted each other like brothers, while my solitude was quite striking. No one came up to me cheerfully or held me to his heart. Nonetheless, because of the length of time I had been on Athos, the passers-by were not completely unknown to me. I had come across such and such a face on a distant track; I thought I remembered a child who I had probably seen in a church, and who was now taking hot coffee to good monks sitting at the back of a shop, robes hitched up over their trousers of rough grey cloth, and warming their fingers, swollen with cold, over a little brazier. I would have found this solitude painful—not a true solitude, more an absence, the beginnings of nonexistence—if the fact that I knew I was on a journey again, and the feeling of drunkenness brought on by the dazzling brightness of the snow had not been enough to fill me with joy.

All the more so since I had just found a thousand drachma note in the depths of a pocket! A thousand drachmas that came from where? A thousand drachmas forgotten since when? It was then I remembered I was very hungry. I did not recognise the innkeeper, and my face seemed unknown to him. It was not the man who had bought my Luftwaffe uniform; that had been a long time ago. But, thank God, the food that was simmering on the antique stoves had not changed: it was well-known for being the best since Saint Athanasius! I feasted on platefuls of lentils, but stubbornly refused the meat they offered me; without quite knowing why, I felt an overwhelming disgust for animal flesh. I was not so fussy about the resinous wine! Around ten o'clock in the morning, slightly drunk, I bought a few things and went back to my table, well-supplied with tea, sugar, bread, a spirit lamp, a warm balaclava and a little metal teapot, which I needed in order to set off alone through the woods to the distant monastery of Esphigmenou, where I had decided to base myself for a while. Leaning back against a wall at the rear of the inn, my favourite spot each time I was in Kariés, how could I doubt it? Once again I had been seized by my obsession for wandering. And this time I had the feeling it was my final expedition. So was I never happy except when travelling? I felt no attachment to anyone or anything, anywhere. Without friends, without religion, without a master, without a child, could I only find peace on the road?

It was a strange destiny. But, I thought in that dark corner at the back of an inn, could I complain about it? Today, my state of perpetual wanderer seemed clearer than ever to me. Yet instead of being weighed down by it, to my great surprise I accepted it enthusiastically. This terrible freedom, this total disengagement and withdrawal, the feeling I increasingly had of time exploding, heralded the imminent AWAKENING. I was in my last incarnation! As old as the world, having probably known everything in many different lives, free at last to go towards the Light, I began to see my solitude, however appalling it might be, as the reward for a very ancient love of God. I was secretly worried by faint forebodings, but they did not frighten me. The idea of ending up on a road, like a fallen beast, my heart broken with fatigue, did not bother me, for there was something of a '*starets*' in me. I wanted to see the sea one last time, even if it was stormy at this time of year; then, via Vatopedi, to get to Esphigmenou. I gathered my belongings and paid my bill.

At the end of the day, after a long walk, I spotted a deserted inlet which I did not know. I stopped and lay down on the sand. The whole of Athos was still white with snow, frozen, except on the shore. It was almost warm beside the foam and the water. The air here smelt of salt and seaweed. Slow, heavy swells lifted up the grey sea; a steady wind created powerful waves … they crashed violently onto the shingle, broke apart and spurted up again as spray: a deafening noise made me drunk with pleasure. I was in no hurry; I gathered some dry wood, lit a fire and sheltered from the wind. I fetched some fresh, slightly salt water from a little stream that made peaceful puddles here and there among the round pebbles, a few steps away from the violent breaking of the waves. I put my metal teapot on the burning embers; lying on the sand, my coat wrapped tightly round me, among a pile of branches, my manuscripts still attached to my belt, I treated myself to some scalding hot, sweet tea while I watched the movement of the sea … happy, with the primitive pleasure of a perpetual nomad!

I had often slept by the waves. At this time of year it was best to get to a monastery before sunset. Reluctantly I stood up; the idea of stopping and making a camp struck deep chords in me, which today sang and echoed loudly in the wind. All things considered: some tea, a bundle of manuscripts, boots … I could not wish for any other possessions than these, which I could easily spread out on the shingle beside a fire, and gather up quickly if I felt the desire to leave. Leaving hot ashes and the imprint of my body behind me on the sand, I walked away from the sea. In the distance it was pounding other shores beneath vast, snow-covered hills over which loomed the summit of Athos, clearer and purer than usual in the depths of the harsh winter. Again I saw the Sacred Mountain in all its grandeur! To travel one last time through this divine land, to die on a path: could I hope for more from my strange destiny?

My path, through the woods very high in the hills, became a simple track used only by the wild boars and the wolves. In a clearing I was able to escape for a moment from the rampant vegetation that covered the foothills of Athos; some good paths showed that there was a monastery nearby … Which one went to Vatopedi? The one I chose led only to deep thickets, dark and sad, where the snow had not yet reached. Night came quickly at the end of December. I sank in above my waist in beds of dead, rotting leaves, and was almost unable to get out. Slipping on the clayey earth I nearly fell into a ravine; I held on to some young trees, which saved me. I was beginning to despair of getting out of the woods, when I spotted the lead cupolas, the roofs and the towers of Vatopedi a hundred metres below me, close to the cypresses by the sea.

Vatopedi: the largest monastery in Athos! I went in as the gate was closing, and a lantern was being lit by an icon of the Virgin. My clothes soaked with snow and mud, my torn boots no longer staying on my feet, I headed through a long, low, damp arch and quickly passed a shop hollowed out of the thickness of the wall, a sort of stall where several monks were buying things before the first night service. Of course, in my pocket I was gripping the parchment that gave me the right to enter all the monasteries of Athos, but I looked so poor that I preferred to hurry on. Suddenly furious with this false modesty, I went no further beneath the sorry archway; I turned on my heel and went up the three steps that led to the narrow shop that was filled with smoke from a paraffin lamp. When I appeared in the doorway, everyone stopped talking: it was obvious I had come from the forests, I was poor! I produced my parchment, which was studied with the greatest care by holding it close to the lamp. So what had been in my mind? The renouncement of all vanity, no doubt! More deeply, the wish to be 'seen' in rags, but seen by human eyes, so much did solitude weigh me down. Misjudged, scorned, but seen! This was mingled with cowardice, the desire to inspire pity, to be given charity and help. And, among the secret mysteries of my insane character there stirred a terrible joy: the pleasure, wholly that of an actor, of appearing in a new guise, with a new mask on my face, the mask of an old man reduced to extreme distress, and whose soul, on the threshold of the Most Holy Eternity, amuses itself with one final metamorphosis after so many others! They handed back my parchment and gave me some tea. Standing in that porter's lodge, which was used as a grocery store and smelt of rancid oil and pepper, I wondered ardently if I had not trodden the boards in at least one of my incarnations? This taste for metamorphoses—how unchristian it was! As death approached, I became more certain that life—my own and others'—is nothing but a dance, a game, masks, apparitions, theatres of the Spirits—and also I felt more close to God, and I will add: loved by God, God's accomplice! I put down my cup. I was given a blessing and allowed to enter. If only in memory of an old tradition, the rich monks of Vatopedi never turned away wanderers.

I went into an outer courtyard. The brightness of the lamps behind small, tightly-closed windows lit up the high walls with their battlements, the well, the scarlet church, the alley-ways, the houses with several storeys, their balconies painted red or blue. Vatopedi was like a large village. You would have thought you were in Old Russia one evening at Christmas; and perhaps it actually was the night before the nativity of the Christians' God, for a furtive excitement, an air of celebration reigned everywhere in this enormous monastery. Monks hurriedly crossed the courtyards, white with snow, pulling down over their brows the black hoods that covered their heads. There was already singing in the church. At its entrance a heavy door curtain was constantly lifted by monks in a hurry to get to their stalls. A thousand candles burnt inside the altar; each time the curtain was pulled aside it was as if the door to an oven, or to heaven, was being opened.

Exhausted after a long walk, yet happy, light-headed with fresh air and cold, I followed them in. A powerful scent of incense and burning wax finally made me drunk, vagabond that I had become. On this night of celebration the tarnished gold of the ancient mosaics shone intensely, coming back to life. The adolescent angels, emerging from the darkness of the domes, answered the call of the flames and the deep, muffled chants, as old as the Near East. Standing in a dark corner, eyes raised towards the painted cupolas, I looked at these young, smiling angels, their wings outspread … the last metamorphosis of the young Helladic gods! For me, Christ Pantocrator was only a more recent manifestation of the divine … among so many others, a mask that belonged to a Christian domain of nightmares and dreams. The GOLD of the icons and the mosaics—and IT ALONE—was perhaps the true face of God.

At dawn, having walked out of the blue-painted postern gate, its lamp extinguished at this time of day, clear air freed me from the smell of wax and filth that permeated Vatopedi.

Once again everything enchanted me, as, with a stout staff in my hand, I climbed the ancient steps leading up through the silent countryside under a wintry, golden, almost red sky. The abandoned *sketes*, the dark ravines, the rushing streams, the old gardens under snow, this was the jungle, and it was not: a dreamland once inhabited by many monks, and now returning to the primordial forest. Here and there were final traces of the work of Byzantine builders, now almost in ruins, and overrun more each year by the spread of elms, cypress and cedars, by landslides, by rain. If the current occupants of Athos were only very simple people, their distant ancestors had known, with a rare skill, how to shape the rock, lay the now displaced paving stones of the mysterious roads that led deep into the undergrowth, how to choose with perfect taste—that of saintly souls—the location of a hermitage, a fountain at the bottom of a charming little valley, a crossing of paths: never, for a thousand years, had the opinion of a woman or that of a common man prevailed on Athos. I saw what man can do when he builds for the gods. It mattered little to me to know that worshippers of the Virgin and of Christ Pantocrator, those two Semites I did not believe in, were in Paradise. All I needed to make me happy was to go ever further into a land of inexpressible, sacred beauty, where the scent of resin from the pines and the hundred-year-old cedars completely intoxicated me.

Everything delighted me in these forests, myself most of all! My freedom, my lack of identity, my guise, my torn boots, my warm woollen coat and the chiming sound made by a metal teapot and an aluminium flask as they banged together at my waist with every step I took, both tied to my leather belt along with a heavy bundle of manuscripts and a spirit lamp. My poverty and my wanderings gave me something of the nature of the sacred. On my own, having met no one since I left Vatopedi, I felt at home in these woods, where for centuries an axe had never fallen on the great trees that had reached gigantic proportions. Athos, incredibly beautiful in the snow, belonged to me alone.

I knew I was lost, but did not let it worry me too much; for on this side of the enchanted thickets the paths were still visible, and all of them led to *sketes* or monasteries. It was not yet noon: a delightful fountain came into view.

No place, in any land of dreams, made you want to stop as much as this one. Icy water flowed from a bronze mask and filled an old marble trough. I laid my bundle of manuscripts on the edge; it was banging against my hip. Dead leaves floated in the clear water, which reflected the sky. The overflow ran into the snow, creating a stream that almost immediately froze solid. In the sleeping countryside, which seemed dead in the heart of winter, I quenched my thirst at the everlasting spring that poured from the smiling bronze lips. There, I washed myself of my fears. I loved this delicious water that came from the depths of the earth; a benign, very holy force issued from this once pagan fountain. I did not know who I was …

and I had no wish to know: was I not simply a soul as old as this ancient spring which had murmured here for thousands of years and, like it, was merely a spell among all the spells of the world?

I stood the spirit lamp on the marble rim. I put some water on to boil, made myself tea, with a few stones piled up round the flame to shelter it from the slight wind. Happy, drunk with living in this sacred land, I breathed in the powerful scent of the great cedars. Jays chattered in the solitary confinement of enormous clumps of green bamboo, an unexpected sight in the snowy woods. Alone in the forest, and in a state of utter enchantment, I did not tire of looking at the old gardens that were returning to wilderness, the white peak of Athos shining like a flawless diamond beyond the hills, and this venerable old fountain, so kindly disposed to me, beside which sang my humble wanderer's tea.

I blew out the flame and waited for my metal teapot to cool down, for being so poor I had no cup. The jays had gone quiet, the sky was turning deep gold, the day was getting on. I drank my tea. In the incredible silence of the forest I gathered up my belongings, my manuscripts, my spirit lamp, my flask, my tin of sugar. Laden like a mule, the whole ensemble rattling and ringing around my waist, my warm balaclava protecting me from the icy evening air, I set off for Esphigmenou, the old monastery where I wished to live in peace.

More than anything I needed rest, food, warmth and—quite humanly—someone to care about me, for I was dying of distress. I had been at Esphigmenou for a month … and had not moved on because of the storms that prevented me setting off, the heavy falls of snow that blocked the roads, and especially because of my determination not to have to go too soon.

A little bedroom in the attic had been put at my disposal. An Ottoman stove, painted sky-blue, took up half the room. A small boy brought me armfuls of logs twenty times a day. My fire roared away non-stop; an unbearable, delightful heat gave me rest from my weariness and, in January, made me leave the window slightly open until after midnight. I was happy, with the heavy happiness of a beast that has found a warm, peaceful corner and does not intend to leave. I scarcely moved from my bed, and slept practically night and day. As for human contact, which would have drawn me out of my solitude, my relationship with the monks was limited to a few words exchanged with the boy or the cook. I was given shelter in a spirit of charity; I was ignored, I was avoided. Besides, Esphigmenou was only a very poor monastery inhabited by five or six monks, as far as I could tell when I went down to the church. The cook was not the one I had known in the time of my youth. The decent man who currently reigned over the ovens had got it into his head, I did not know why, that he was dealing with a person of importance. I had not put him straight about his pleasant error, which was worth a clean little room to me, but there was a drawback: he absolutely insisted that I have my meals "in the drawing room", not in his kitchen, whose healthy warmth and lovely disorder appealed to me more than the dusty pedestal tables and pious lithographs of the drawing room. All the more so since it was freezing cold in there! The child lit a poor little blaze which went out almost immediately. I did not mind; once I had swallowed the last mouthful I went back to bed.

No doubt I had to sleep before the Awakening! Get my strength back before passing across the final threshold! I had not attempted to see the Clear Primordial Light again, whose memory was usually wiped from my soul while I slept. I had long since given up the search for a master; I loved Athos, I loved Esphigmenou, and saw nothing beyond that. Every afternoon I made some tea in my room, my spirit lamp standing on the sill of my window, which looked out onto the courtyard. At this time of year night fell quickly. I lit a candle, I reread my manuscripts, the tale of my final wanderings, what I had foreseen, put down in writing, and which was actually happening to me. I waited for the next part, without quite believing in it. And yet, if it were true! At six o'clock the child brought me new logs. I stuffed my Ottoman stove, I ate supper "in the drawing room", then slipped between my sheets. I listened to the sound of the sea and the wind ... Continual storms battered the north coast of Athos; as Esphigmenou stood right on the shore, a few steps from the tide, the spray lashed against the high walls; the strongest waves beat violently against our stones, shaking the monastery from cellar to attic. It was a constant uproar that deafened me, so much so that it sent me to sleep. Window panes shattered, gusts of wind blew along the great corridors, the sea kept on roaring. I fell asleep, listening to the terrible storms that made me drunk with happiness.

So was it very close to my end that I met my master, who I had lost hope of ever seeing? One morning as I was wandering in the snowy courtyard, a monk who I had merely glimpsed in the half-darkness of the church gestured to me to follow him. He opened the door of a little chapel. It was a sort of storeroom of marvels where extraordinary treasures had been amassed … as elsewhere in the world you pile up logs. More than a hundred icons of venerable age, hanging on nails, gleamed gently in peaceful shadow, their calm splendour rivalling the pure brightness of the snow. The place smelt of incense, wax and good painting, for that has a smell, as does holiness! And back then, people knew how to paint! The quality of the golds, turned brown by time, of the ochres, the reds; the sweetness of the materials used, exquisite, divine, hard as enamel, sometimes the colour of ivory; the delicacy of the drawing, whose geometry could not be bettered, all made me forget the nearby commotion of the water, when I realised that 'he' was watching me, keys in hand. An ageless man, not so very old, with long, thinning hair gathered into a chignon at the nape of the neck. On Athos I had only come across stupid people, but his handsome face expressed only intelligence, a wild and loving kindness. Was this my master? He met my gaze openly, without avoiding my unspoken questions. I was waiting for a word from him, a gesture. He stayed silent and continued to watch me closely. I was sure: he KNEW who I was … In his eyes I saw an ancient understanding mingled with astonishment, reproach, anger. Then he was carried away by his affection for me; he smiled. He was about to speak: he KNEW where I really came from … He preferred to say nothing. I was convinced that he was deciding, reluctantly, to leave me to my strange destiny, not knowing what to say to a being who was not like anyone, and whose presence here seemed unbelievable. His beautiful eyes dimmed. All I saw in front of me now was no more than a monk, like all the rest, in a hurry to lock the door, to get back to his saucepans, almost a simpleton. But I was certain of it: he was 'playing the fool' out of humility, and especially to disappoint me, to bring me back to my solitude and make me despair.

His good colleagues also worked at it in their own way. A mule-train, taking advantage of an obvious break in the snow storms, had just arrived from Kariés and was leaving the next day. With the mule-drivers I again saw the learned doctor who had treated my burns. He was hurrying to the bedside of an old monk who was slowly dying. They gave me to understand, tactfully, that since I was only a stranger, as well as suspected of being rather unchristian, I could not stay on at Esphigmenou any longer; in short, I was asked to clear off. This time I regretted that a decent illness did not keep me bedridden, obliging these fine folk to take me in for good. But annoyingly I was as fit as a fiddle, apart from a slight breathlessness, which I was used to and which no longer worried me.

We mounted at dawn. The mules, nostrils steaming, stamped the ground with their hoofs and shook their bells. Hippocrates opened a black umbrella to protect himself from the snow and wind. I hugged myself tightly in my woollen overcoat and we set off, sometimes walking quickly to warm ourselves up and relieve the strain on our animals, sometimes cantering along with a good jab of the spurs.

By sunset we were at Kariés. Once the mules had been left at the inn I headed for the nearby monastery of Koutloumousiou, where I hoped to spend several days, perhaps more, since the harsh winter weather forced the monks to show a little more pity than usual towards the unfortunate. I was starting to think like a vagrant, and my Slavonic soul was actually quite comfortable with my being utterly destitute. At the entrance to the orchard I stopped to get my breath back.

Leaning my elbows on a low stone wall where I had put my manuscripts, I stared for a long time at the snow-covered countryside. The sky had cleared. The transparent air, tinged from pink to nocturnal blue, and gold above the dark forests, was slowly getting darker. One star glowed beside the white marble of Athos. A vast, almost Asian landscape, I thought: Japanese. The bright summit of the Holy Mountain 'reminded' me of Fujiyama! I walked up to the entrance of the monastery, crossing the orchard whose trees had been stripped bare by winter.

I got a rather poor reception. I ate in the kitchens. I was told that I could not be given shelter for more than one night. However Slavonic I might be, my beggar-like condition then dawned on me in all its horror. On top of that I was exhausted by a long journey. Unable to hold back my tears I went out into the courtyard. I leant against a wall, my chest shaken by uncontrollable sobs. My heart was breaking! A violent pain was crushing my throat and my left shoulder; I fell into the snow and the mud. A sharp, unbearable pain! For a whole quarter of an hour, beside myself with agony and fear, I moaned in the darkness. The pain eased off but I could feel my blood freezing; life was ebbing away from my limbs. I was cold, very cold. I had reached the end of a life: I was going to die. Heavily I got to my feet, my clothes soaked with mud, and headed for the church, drawn by the gold of the candlelit icons, drawn by the ever-more beautiful and solemn chants, which called me to them and which were helping me to die.

What a strange religion mine is, with no God but the Clear Primordial Light whose admirable reflection is GOLD, I thought, already outside myself, no longer able to stand up straight, one shoulder leaning against a scarlet column. GOLD fascinated me. A great shaft of light suddenly passed through my mind: I had thought I was very old, as old as the world. I was convinced I had been a magician, an alchemist in Byzantium, a monk in Russia, on Athos, in Asia … TIME suddenly turned upside down so violently that I almost passed out. ON THE CONTRARY, I came from the FUTURE … and I was now exploring humanity's past, some profound regions of the psyche—both human and divine—before returning to the civilization of the stars, of light and of gold, my real homeland and my true time! I came from the future. The monk at Esphigmenou had known this, but he had not wanted to tell me.

They thought the man who collapsed in a corner of the church was drunk, the man who they carried to a bed and comforted; a vagrant who was given hot soup and tea … who got out of bed as the night ended and set off along the paths which led towards the bright marble summit of Athos.

I knew I was close to death. I did not want to meet my end among Christians. I could hear a call that came from the stars and from space. I was heading for the heights, towards the sky, still dark with night and scattered with stars. I climbed the stone steps with difficulty, short of breath, my heart broken. I wanted to die gazing at the rising sun, in the peace and silence of the high snowy slopes. I began to hurry, irresistibly drawn by the sky. I walked quickly, without feeling tired. I looked at my reflection in a little fountain: the old man's mask that had covered my face had disappeared. I was young again! I set off once more through the sleeping woods, and did not stop until I reached the edge of a precipice: beyond, there was only emptiness.

There I sat down to die, my hands resting on my thighs, my body upright. I waited calmly for THE AWAKENING. Day was breaking, intensely blue in the infinite space.

Before me rose the sharp peak of the Sacred Mountain, solitary as an island above the banks of mist that hid the valleys. Delicately, the first rays of the sun touched the crystal-clear marble. THE AWAKENING! But who was it who was dying? I was withdrawing peacefully from an old dream … and I smiled after my long wanderings in the archaic depths of the human and divine soul. I soared into the sky. I saw God,

THE LIVING GOLD THAT SINGS
AT THE HEART OF AN INCREDIBLE
SILENCE.

Port of the Monastery of Grégorios

AFTERWORD

François Augiéras
Hospice de Domme 24

3 August 1969

Dear Jean Chalon,

I have sent Etienne Lalou a 'note for insertion' useful for an excellent understanding of A Journey to Mount Athos. *Here it is:*

The theme of this novel, A Journey to Mount Athos, *is that of a stay in the Land of the Spirits, according to the strictest Buddhist or Pythagorean orthodoxy.*

Our traveller, who is dead, can be reincarnated immediately: the daughter of Ierissos—the village of young, desirable women—offers to make him "a fine child", or to put it plainly, to return him to the world of mortals. Our hero, whose soul appears old and wise already, decides to venture further into the Land of the Spirits. So he sets out by sea, heading for the Holy Mountain. There he finds happiness, the consequence of his past actions, of his deepest tendencies, a paradise that he is sure he has been to before: a strange paradise where at any given moment time seems disconnected, broken apart, changed as a result of being close to the Divine. In the world beyond he will again meet people he has loved in former times, elsewhere … He will hear the final echoes of his previous lives.

After many charms and enchantments he will have to choose: either return to live among the living, or awaken from his own death and attain the Clear Primordial Light so often mentioned in the Bardo-Thödol, *the* Tibetan Book of the Dead. *Severely burnt, purified by suffering, he withdraws into the region of caves. He will become aware of his true, cosmic* SELF, *which is simply an archetype as old as the world, which would have interested*

Jung. In the final pages he will resume his wanderings on the Holy Mountain until the moment when, all karma exhausted and time destroyed—for a moment he will even believe that he comes from the future—he finally returns to the Clear Primordial Light: the living Gold that sings at the heart of an incredible silence.

This entirely initiatory and symbolic book ends with this return to Energy, to the Pure State … which men call God.

What do you think of my note for insertion? I think I have set out my plan clearly, in a few words … without weighing down the charms and enchantments of the Holy Mountain with too much 'philosophy'.

[…] The manuscript of A Journey to Mount Athos *is yours; I would be glad to give it to you when you come to the Dordogne. Naturally, I can send it to you if our meeting this summer turns out to be impossible.*

That meeting did turn out to be impossible. It was the time of my life when Natalie Clifford Barney, Florence Jay-Gould and Louise de Vilmorin took up a lot of my time. Anxious to collect together the memories of their past and present glories, I was never able to escape, even for a weekend, to meet this man François Augiéras who lived in a cave in the Dordogne, where he practised strange rites that he described in *Domme ou un essai d'occupation.* And yet to me he seemed like a master, since he was free to use his time in whatever way he chose, while I was, and still am, the slave of my schedule. He taught me that you can exist on nothing. He lived on tea and burning incense. He wrote me letters that brought me a great breath of fresh air very different from the one I breathed in Parisian salons.

I owed my discovery of his books, such as *Le Voyage des morts* [Voyage of the Dead], to Jacques Brenner. Reading them led me into unknown territory completely different from the world I knew. They aroused in me a fascination mixed with fear. If I use my own personal example, it is because I challenge you to embark upon Augiéras' work, and especially *A Journey to Mount Athos*, without immediately feeling that fascination and that fright, when confronted with universes where only a rare elect ever venture. My relationship with François Augiéras was therefore limited to a correspondence that began in 1968 and ended in 1971. In his letters, the author of *Le Vieillard et l'enfant* [The Old Man and the Child], that same *Vieillard et l'enfant* which he had published under the pseudonym of Abdallah Chaamba, spoke of the difficulties of living, writing and above all getting published.

Two publishers, who shall remain nameless, had just turned down *A Journey to Mount Athos*. This double rejection had affected Augiéras. He was convinced that he was a cursed writer, which alas was only too true … ! Despairing of getting anywhere, he entrusted me with a typed copy of *Mount Athos*. As soon as I read it, and loved it passionately, I passed it on to Etienne Lalou, who was then publishing director of Flammarion. Forty-eight hours were all Lalou needed to recognise that this book was a masterpiece of the unexpected. But is it not true that all of Augiéras' work is unexpected, unique in its genre, set apart in our century?

Augiéras himself felt he was different, and very conscious of his singularity. On 20th March 1970, he wrote to me, "*Sometimes it seems to me that I am a distant star […] That is to say, if you like, a Quasar: those stars that are difficult to locate anywhere, with their highly enigmatic signals, and about which all theories are possible".* He constantly kept his distance from human beings and, the minute he was able, set off into wide open spaces. Such behaviour, such a need for escape, is perhaps explained in a paragraph of Forster's *A Passage to India*: "The old, very old malaise that gnaws at the heart of every civilization: snobbery, the desire for wealth and for honoured accessories; it is to escape that, rather than the temptations of the flesh that saints withdraw into the Himalayas". Augiéras was not a saint. He simply loved to withdraw into his internal Himalayas. He also loved to surround himself with mystery, and the biographical note that accompanied *A Journey to Mount Athos* on its publication taught me more about its author than months of correspondence:

François Augiéras was born in 1925, in Rochester (United States). His father was a French pianist and his mother a Polish émigrée. He returned to France after the death of his father and spent his adolescence in Périgord. Abandoning his studies at the age of fifteen, he quite quickly turned to a sort of wandering.

The discreet and accurate summary, "a sort of wandering", is admirable. Augiéras' life and books are a series of various wanderings in France, North Africa and Greece. Each of his pages is in itself a voyage, and often an initiatory one. In it you are hungry, you are thirsty, you make love to forget hunger and thirst, then, with superb ease, you move from the pleasures of the body to the ecstasies of the spirit.

In *A Journey to Mount Athos*, François Augiéras reveals himself as a pilgrim who is able to attract the company of young cherubs, and old hermits whose beards are as long as their experience. He comes, he goes, he picks the fruits that appear as if by some miracle along his way, and savours them with a sensual pleasure that does not prevent him from being lucid. He reached his Promised Land, he finally found his country: Athos. "On Athos, through lack of food, through want, you were only too liable to stray into delicious errors and, because of solitude, to *find everything within yourself*."

It is I who have emphasized that phrase, *find everything within yourself*, in which we can recognise echoes of the most ancient wisdom. Thus François Augiéras, who in his lifetime was sometimes taken for a madman, was a wise man. Like a wise man he died, detached from everything, at the Hospice de Domme, in 1971.

One could put this epitaph on his tombstone. It was written by Jean Cocteau for himself, and can be found at the end of his *Requiem*:

Halt pilgrim my voyage
Took me from danger to danger
It is right that people should dream of me
After staring at me.

And now it is time to restore François Augiéras' face to him, like a star, or an underground beacon …

JEAN CHALON
14th September 1987